Contents

Misfits, Monsters, and	1
Prologue	4
Chapter One	5
Chapter Two	14
Chapter Three	23
Chapter Four	32
Chapter Five	44
Chapter Six	50
Chapter Seven	56
Chapter Eight	62
Chapter Nine	72
Chapter Ten	82
Chapter Eleven	92
Chapter Twelve	101
Chapter Thirteen	105
Chapter Fourteen	109
Chapter Fifteen	120
Chapter Sixteen	128
Chapter Seventeen	132
Chapter Eighteen	136

Chapter Nineteen	147
Chapter Twenty	150
Chapter Twenty-One	157
Epilogue	161
About The Author	163

Misfits, Monsters, and Mayhem

Wendy Dunkin

Copyright W.E.Dunkin 2023

This book is a work of fiction. Names, charaters, places and incidents either are products of the author's imagination or are used fictitiously. Any resemblance to actual events or locales or persons, living or dead, is entirely coincidental. All rights reserved. Except as permitted under the U.S. Copyright Act of 1976, no part of this publication may be reproduced, distributed or transmitted in any form or by any means, or stored in a database or retrieval system, without the prior written permission of the publisher.

This book is dedicated to my beautiful children. Yes, you're grown-ups, married, and having babies of your own, but you'll always be my babies, my legacy, and my greatest contribution to the world. You were my first real and honest loves and always one half my heart, one half my soul. Live your dreams, laugh often, love completely. Love you both to the moon and back!

Prologue

"So, what do you think we should do, Frank?"

Frank played with the Velcro strip on his wrist as he considered his answer.

"I'm telling you! We need to get with the council on this. This is beyond our abilities. They have the resources to investigate. They should be involved."

"No, Guiseppe. We cannot afford to trust anyone from the council until we know for sure who is behind this. Anna's brother is investigating. We can trust him and him only," countered Jeremiah.

Frank still fiddled with the strip on his wrist. "I think….."

"There's no thinking about it. I agree with Guiseppe. This is beyond our abilities, and we need to work with the authorities."

"Cyrus, please let Frank speak."

Frank looked at each of the people in the room and said, "While I agree we shouldn't involve ourselves with the council or any other member of law enforcement besides Derek at this time, we do need help. We need to keep our eyes and ears open and watch our backs, keep an eye on our families. Someone is taking these people and we need to find out who and why."

Chapter One

I awoke to the early morning sun streaming through the window blinds and a dog breathing in my face. As soon as I cracked an eye open, I was rewarded with slobbery dog kisses.

"Ok Gracie girl. I'm awake. Let's get your breakfast and let you outside."

Gracie jumped down from the side of the bed and headed out of the bedroom toward the kitchen, tail held high and wagging furiously.

I sat up and swung my feet over the side of the bed. I yawned, stretched, slipped into my house shoes, grabbed my robe, and padded into the kitchen behind her to make her breakfast.

Gracie was dancing around my feet in eager anticipation of her food. After taking care of her, I poured myself a cup of coffee.

I checked my cell phone and noticed a missed call and a voicemail. I dialed in to hear my grandmother's voice.

"Bethie Lynn, hi! It's me. Grandma Gloria. Down in Florida. I need your opinion on something. Call me when you get a chance, okay? Love you."

Grandma calling for my opinion was a normal thing—unlike Grandma who was anything but normal. How one little old lady could possibly come up with some of the wild ideas that my grandmother did is way above my pay grade.

I sighed, wondering what she had gotten up to this time. It wouldn't surprise me if I got a call one day from Grams needing bail money. Yes, this was a real possibility with my grandmother, and it had almost happened last month.

I dialed Gram's number, and she answered on the first ring. It sounded like a huge party was happening in the background.

"Grams, where are you?" I shouted into the phone, praying she hadn't decided to start another topless protest gathering.

Those pictures on the news of my grandmother letting it all hang out were likely to give me nightmares for years to come, even though the bad parts had been blurred out. Most people have to seek therapy because of their parents. My parents were great. If I ever had to go to therapy, you can thank my grandmother.

"Hi Sweetie! We're at a rave party. You know, one of those rowdy secret parties with booze, music, hot guys, lots of dancing. The kids threw one and invited me and my crew."

Her crew?

"Yes, Grams, I know what a rave is. The question is, what are you doing at one, especially this early?"

I could just picture my grandmother and her 'crew' prancing around with glow in the dark necklaces, drinking strange cocktail combinations, and dancing with guys a quarter of their ages. I don't understand how she and her older friends could stand the noise from the blaring, raucous music unless they had their hearing aids turned down or off.

"Oh, you know me. The OPG. We've been going all night! I even got to try my hand at being the deejay for a spell." (OPG stands for 'original party girl', in case you were wondering.)

All night? Didn't most people her age go to bed at like 4:00 p.m.? Wait, those are *normal older people.*

Grams was the epitome of 'cool grandma'. In her younger days, she and my grandpa hitchhiked to Woodstock. They ended up getting picked up by Ritchie Havens and she, somehow, made it onto the stage with Jimmy Hendrix and Jefferson Airplane to sing a couple of songs with both.

She'd hung out in the Haight-Ashbury district and met Janis Joplin. She was the one who convinced Janis to paint her Porsche with the psychedelic paint job the car was famous for.

Jim Morrison from The Doors was so smitten with her that, when he sang the Van Morrison song 'Gloria', he dedicated it to her every time. He had a huge crush on her. She thought he was a pest.

She'd met my grandpa at the Monterey International Pop Festival and married him after only being together three days. Grams called him her kindred free-spirited soul mate.

She loved to tell everyone the story of my mother being born in the back of someone's VW 'love van', much to my mother's embarrassment. That embarrassment is only second to her real birth name, which she had legally changed to Donna upon turning 18. Please never make the mistake of asking her what she changed it from. I can't afford to bail two relatives out of jail.

After Mom was born, Grams and Gramps decided it was time to settle down. Gramps got a job at the post office, they purchased a modest ranch-style house in a suburban neighborhood, and Grams stayed home to raise my mom.

She and Gramps still had fun together, like their yearly trips to Sturgis on my grandpa's Harley-Davidson—more pictures I don't ever want to be privy to again--but they took the responsibility of parenting seriously.

When my grandpa passed away about ten years ago, Grams was shattered. After the funeral, she bought an open-ended ticket to India and was gone for several months. She hadn't mentioned anything to anyone that she was leaving, other than a quick note saying, 'I'll be back'. She just hopped onto a plane and was gone. We later found out she'd gone to an ashram to help her deal with the grief of losing Gramps.

These days she and her like-minded girlfriends hung out down in Florida with the local college kids who thought she was the coolest old lady ever. She was 74 years old and showed no signs of slowing down.

My dad often joked that my mother was adopted. She's straight-laced and normal. Grams calls her boring—behind her back, of course. If my mother knew about half of the conversations I have with my grandmother and all the wacky things I've had to talk her out of from time to time, she would move my grandmother into a convent before my grandmother could do her next body shot.

"Grams, can you go somewhere quieter? I can barely hear you."

There was a bit of shuffling, then the sound of a door closing. While the noise was still there, it was muffled enough that I could hear my grandmother.

"How's that, sweetheart?"

"Better. Now, Grams, what do you need my opinion on?"

Grams started clicking her dentures around, a sure sign she was going to suggest doing something outrageous.

"Well, I'm thinking about moving. I've been invited to join this other community that sounds much more akin to my free-spirited ways. There's a bunch of people my age living there, and everybody pulls together to make it a self-sufficient community. It would be a lot cheaper for me than my current apartment."

"Uh, Grams...."

"We live off the proceeds from the farming we do."

"Hold on, Grams, what type of 'farming' are we talking about?"

"Oh, this and that. You know. Like mushrooms. And pot. What else? Pot is legal now. Somewhere at least. Go figure! So, anyway, in this community, we don't have the need for a bunch of fancy stuff. Clothes, shoes, money. Nuh uh. None of that is required. And you can only live there if you were invited. Not just anyone can join."

"Grams, no! You are not moving to a commune of old naked mushroom and pot farming hippies!"

The thought of a bunch of naked old people roaming around made me want to gouge my eyes out with a toothpick. It was yet another series of images that would stay in my brain forever.

"But, sweetie, haven't you heard anything I said? It's more me. This stodgy old community I'm in now doesn't let me breathe. You're pretty uptight for someone so young. I think you've been spending too much time with your mom. You need to let your hair down. Let loose!"

"Grams, no. If Mom gets word of this, you'll be living in her spare bedroom. You think you can't breathe now? No more parties, no more drunken karaoke, no more streaking through the streets, and certainly no more topless protests."

"Oh, that was big fun. But yes, there is that I guess. Your mother seems to enjoy ruining all my fun."

"Gloria, come on, you're missing all the action! We're getting ready to do body shots off that hot bartender! Let's go!"

"Alright, sweetie. Thanks for the chat. I've gotta go."

"Grams!"

"Don't worry. I heard what you said. No new community. It would probably be boring hanging around all those old people anyway. Love you!" <click>

I swear, trying to keep up with my grandmother sometimes was like trying to corral a herd of two-year-olds in a candy store.

I had no sooner set my phone down than it rang again. Thinking it was my grandmother calling back, I answered without looking to see who was calling.

"Hello my beautiful wife."

Crap! Could this day get any more frustrating? My ex-husband.

"I'm not your wife, for the ten thousandth time. What do you want, Jason?"

"I've been thinking about you all week. You know I love you. Why won't you let me come back?"

"We're divorced, Jason. The ink is dry on the decree. We're done."

"Oh baby, come on. You know I love you. There's no one else for me but you."

"Yeah, me and any other girl who comes within fifty miles of your line of vision. No thanks!"

"Baby, those other girls meant nothing to me. You know that. You complete me. I haven't been the same without you."

"No, Jason. We are done. Finished. Over. Besides, what happened to Candie? I thought she was your next forever?"

"Eh she wasn't nothing to me. Not like you."

"She left you, huh?"

"Yeah, but it was for the best. She knew she could never hold a candle to you. You're one grade-A classy broad, baby. I tried so hard to get her to hang up her pasties and G-string and settle down with me. She told me to drop dead and threw her G-string at me! Can you believe it?"

Oh good lord! What is it about today with people and over sharing information? I might call a therapist after all. Of course, the way my day was starting out, I may need an entire team of mental health professionals.

"Goodbye, Jason."

"No, baby, wait!"

I hung up.

Jason and I had been married for almost three years when I discovered he was a card-carrying gold star rewards member of the local strip club. Yeah, you got points for every time you visited that you could cash in for free drinks, lap dances, and the like.

Candie was one of the dancers and the final nail in the coffin of my sham marriage. I also found out Jason was quite well known to a few of the dancers. Must have been all those points he racked up.

I can't believe I never saw through his fake good boy façade. He just oozed charm, class, and good manners when I met him in college.

I was nineteen and in my second year at Missouri State, majoring in accounting. Jason was 20, also a second-year student majoring in business management. We had a business accounting class together and he sat next to me, introducing himself to me on the first day.

He was tall and slender with soft brown hair, cut and styled perfectly. His green eyes lit up when he smiled or laughed, and he was relaxed, charming and confident. He dressed impeccably, never showing up to class looking anything but put together. We started out as study partners then one day, Jason invited me to lunch.

He was a complete gentleman, opening doors, holding my chair for me. We talked for three hours and found so many things we had in common. We talked about family, places we'd been, future goals. I'll admit, I was falling hard.

Before the end of the year, we were a couple. We stayed together, marrying shortly after we both graduated from college. I'd gotten a job with a major accounting firm in the county; he'd been hired as a department manager for a moving company.

I'd been on my job for a little over a year when they started downsizing, and I was one of the first employees to be let go. Jason was super supportive and convinced me I should get my C.P.A. degree and start my own accounting business. He had recently been promoted to department director at the company he worked for, so money wasn't really an issue.

With his help, I launched my accounting business. It was slow going the first few months, but it seemed like no time before I had a steady stream of regular clients.

One day, the mask slipped, the jig was up, and he showed me just what a slime ball he really is. It was my birthday and I'd gone out for a birthday lunch with several of my girlfriends. Jason was taking me out that evening for dinner at my favorite restaurant in the city.

When I came home from lunch, I walked in on him and Candie *in flagrante* on the couch in our living room. I left our apartment, went straight to the lawyer's office and filed for divorce.

I moved my things out of our apartment the next day, packed them into a U-Haul trailer and drove away with no particular destination in mind. I stopped to gas up my car about three hours later and went inside to grab a cold drink.

As I came out of the gas station, an old woman was standing by the corner of the building holding a puppy. I walked over to her, and she smiled as I petted the wiggling little ball of fur.

"Looks like you've made a friend," the old woman said to me and smiled. "She's the last one I have from the litter if you'd like to take her."

I debated for a few minutes. Jason didn't want animals. He said they were too much responsibility and too messy. That should have been my first clue. Our apartment didn't allow pets anyway.

It was when the puppy looked up at me with such hopeful eyes, almost as if she understood what the woman had said, that I was hooked. I took her and named her Gracie for her varying shades of gray fur.

I stopped for lunch in the quaint little town. The waitress, an older, grandmotherly type, noticed the trailer hooked behind my car and asked where I was heading. Maybe it was stress, maybe it was fatigue, but I spilled the whole sordid story to the kind waitress. She patted my hand then told me about an apartment over a garage that was available if I was interested in living here in the town.

I thought it over for a few minutes then decided I'd stay. Gertie, the waitress, called the owner, who then came to the diner to take me to the property. I asked him if he allowed pets. He told me he did, so I signed the lease and settled in.

Jason, not one to give up easily, has called me more times in the year since I left than he did during our entire six years together.

My cell phone rang again. Of course, it was Jason, who showed up as *Asshat* on my display. (See what I mean?) I pushed ignore and put the phone down on the counter.

"Come on, Gracie. Let's go for a ride. It's a beautiful day and I need to get out of here for a while."

Gracie, always ready for a ride, woofed her agreement. I got dressed, grabbed her leash, and headed for the car

Chapter Two

One of the best things about the town I lived in was the fact that you could go from the town to the country in minutes.

Gracie and I decided to cruise the two-lane highway out of town and into the more rural parts. Occasionally we'd pass another vehicle, but we mostly had the entire road to ourselves.

We stopped at McGoogle's Farm Center which sold everything from farming equipment to groceries. Good thing too, seeing as it was the only place around for miles. I purchased a sandwich and bottled water for myself and some home baked dog treats and a second bottle of water for Gracie. I kept a collapsible dog dish in my car for just these occasions so Gracie would have something to drink water from if we were out and about.

We were about 20 miles outside of the town we lived in when Gracie started whining and prancing around the back seat. She alternated between this and pawing at my arm.

"Do you need a potty break, girl? Let me find a good place to pull over to let you out."

I saw a road ahead and signaled to turn. I figured once Gracie had relieved herself, we could hop back on the road.

I turned off the highway and drove a little bit down the road trying to find a safe place to pull over. Soon the tree-lined road opened up to a small town. Gracie pawed at my arm again.

"Okay, girl. I think I see a place just up here."

To the right was a small dog park. People were out with their dogs, playing frisbee, some dogs were playing in the doggy fountain. Other dogs were laying in the shade on blankets, napping. I pulled into the parking lot and shut the car off. I got out of the car and opened the back door to let Gracie out and led her over to the designated potty area.

Once Gracie was done and I'd cleaned up after her, we wandered over to the recreation area and sat down on a bench to watch the other dogs. I opened one of the waters to give Gracie a drink in her portable bowl, then opened the wrapper of my sandwich. I had just finished eating when a little girl walked up to me, smiling shyly.

"Hello, ma'am. My name is Daisy. What's your name? Is this your daughter?"

I smiled back at the little girl, a little confused as to why she thought Gracie was my daughter but chalked it up to a small child's imagination.

"Hi Daisy. I'm Beth and this is Gracie. She is my dog and probably my best friend in the whole world."

Daisy continued to smile and asked, "What kind of dog is she? Does she change into something else? May I pet her? I wish I could have a dog."

Okay, these questions are getting a little bit strange, but it has been one of those days. What would Gracie change into?

"Gracie is an Australian shepherd mix and yes, you may pet her. I think she'd like that."

Daisy crouched down to eye level with Gracie and started stroking her soft, thick fur. Gracie was in Heaven.

"So, Daisy, do you live here?"

"Yes ma'am. I live over on Midnight Ridge with my mommy, daddy, and my brother. That's my brother over there with those other boys. He's in third grade. I wanted to play with them, but they were being stinky boys."

I looked in the direction Daisy was pointing but didn't see any kids, just a group of dogs playing with a tennis ball. Maybe Daisy was just pointing out into the park, not to a specific place.

"They told me I have girl cooties. I said, 'Nuh uh'. Then they told me I have fleas. I told them I didn't either because Mama had just given me my weekly flea bath, but they still wouldn't let me play, so I came over to talk to you. You don't think I have fleas, do you?"

Fleas? What? This was one very imaginative little girl!

"No, honey. Boys can just be so silly sometimes."

"My mommy and daddy named me Daisy because they said I was born smiling and happy. Just like a real daisy. I'm in first grade. Do you go to school? This is my new dress. Isn't it pretty? Do you have kids? Where do you live?"

I'd forgotten how quickly little kids could fire off questions and change the subject without warning. She was shifting gears so fast, my brain was going to short circuit.

"That's a very pretty dress. I'm all finished with school. I don't have any kids right now. It's just Gracie and me. We live in Glen Oaks. Gracie and I decided to take a little drive, but Gracie needed a potty break so here we are."

"Oh. I think you should move here. You'd really like it. The people are nice, and Gracie could make some new doggie friends."

"That would be really nice honey, but Gracie and I have a home and people who would be sad to see us go."

Daisy's tiny face fell a little before she said, "Oh. Well, my mommy sells houses, and she could find you a new home. My daddy is a 'torney. I'm not sure what that is. I could be your new friend. And Gracie's too, as long as you don't tell me I have cooties or fleas. That wouldn't be very nice."

Before I could respond, a tall dark-haired woman, dressed in a polo shirt, khaki pants, and athletic shoes approached us.

"Daisy, honey. Are you bothering this nice lady?"

"No ma'am. This is my new friend Beth and her doggie Gracie. She doesn't have any kids yet and she says I don't have fleas or cooties like Micah said."

The woman let out a nervous laugh, then reached out her hand toward me.

"Hi! I'm Anna Wolfsbane, Daisy's mom. I'm so sorry if she's bothering you. We don't get many visitors here."

I shook her outstretched hand and said, "Hi Anna. She's no bother. She's been very polite. And she has quite the imagination!"

Anna smiled as Daisy said, "Momma, I've told Miss Beth she should move here. I think she'd really like it. It's a nice town to live in, isn't it Momma?"

"Honey, that's up to her. I'm sure she has a home. Now run along and play. We have to take your brother to his game in a little while." Daisy scampered off to play with some of the other kids.

"She's such a cute little girl," I told Anna.

"Yes, but I'm afraid once she sinks her teeth into an idea, she won't let go. I'm so sorry if she made you uncomfortable. She can be quite a chatterbox! But she's right. This is a great town to live in. Everyone looks out for everyone, and you don't have to worry about a lot of the problems other towns have. If you ever decide to look, I'm a realtor and I can show you some terrific places."

"Thanks, Anna. I'll keep it in mind. Right now, I'm renting a small apartment in Glen Oaks. It's a three-room rental above a garage, but it works for what I need. I'm recently divorced, and I own an accounting business, which I run from home. And I'm not sure why I suddenly started telling a stranger my life story. Forgive me."

Anna laughed and said, "It's the town. Seems to have that effect on people it likes. It's almost as if the town decides who would be a good fit here. It was nice meeting you and I'm sorry, but I must run. My son has a Little League game I have to get him to. Let me give you my card in case you're ever interested in buying a house."

Anna reached into the small clutch she was carrying and handed me a business card with Full Moon Realty printed on it, along with her contact information.

"It was nice meeting you too, Anna. I'll keep you in mind."

"Thanks! Safe travel. Take care!"

Anna walked away to gather up her kids and I stood to discard the trash from my sandwich and collect Gracie. As I looked down, I noticed Gracie was no longer sitting by the bench. I looked around the park, not seeing her anywhere. The area was fenced in so she couldn't have gotten out, but panic started setting in. Maybe someone opened the gate and she slipped out?

"Gracie. Gracie! Come on girl. We have to go."

I started walking around the park, searching frantically for my dog. I whistled, which usually brought her running, but not this time. I did notice some of the people in the dog park, along with their dogs, stopped as soon as I whistled and looked at me with rapt attention. Umm....okay.

I started walking around asking some of the others in the park if they'd seen Gracie. No one had.

I was near tears when I happened to look across the street. Gracie was sitting on the sidewalk in front of one of the local businesses. Relief tamped down the panic as I left the park and crossed over to where my dog was waiting.

"Gracie! You scared the crap out of me! How did you get out and what are you doing here?"

Gracie just looked at me, looked up at the window of the business, then looked back at me.

I looked up at the window of the business, trying to figure out what had caught my dog's attention.

Full Moon Realty was painted on the window in bold letters.

Gracie looked up at me, pawing at my leg in the process.

"I see. You've made a new friend and now you don't want to leave. But we have to go home."

Gracie whined and stood up on her hind legs, pawing at the window. I looked at the paper she was pawing toward. It was a listing for a three bedroom, two- and one-half bath home in the town. It was reasonably priced too, well within my budget.

I allowed myself to dream for just a second, then sighed and picked up Gracie's leash.

"Yes, love. It would be nice to have a real house, but now isn't a good time."

Gracie looked at me then asked, "Why not?"

"Uhhhh. I think the stress of losing you has gone to my head. I could have sworn you just spoke to me. Hahaha. But that's not possible. Dogs don't talk. Someone must be playing a joke on me. Okay not funny. You can come out now."

I started looking around for a hidden speaker or a child hiding behind something.

Gracie looked up at me and said, "That was me and yes, I can talk. This town is the perfect place for us. That house is just what we need."

"Yeahhhhh. Okay. I think it's time for us to go Gracie. The sun must be getting to me. Or I'm having a stroke. Do I smell burnt toast? I think I do. Yep, I'm having a stroke."

We headed back to the car. I got Gracie loaded and sat in the driver's seat. I put the key in the ignition but didn't start the car. What the actual crap? Was I dreaming? Talking dogs, right! What's next? Unicorns and leprechauns?

I looked up and down the street just in case a leprechaun riding on the back of a unicorn decided to walk by. It wouldn't surprise me at this point.

"Beth, trust me. You aren't having a stroke. Yes, I can talk. I know it's something you could never have imagined but it's true. Now, let's talk about our new house."

I turned in the driver's seat to look in the back seat at my dog. Okay, I'll play along. I was convinced someone was playing a joke on me. Dogs do not talk! I decided to test this theory. I made sure the radio was off and the doors and windows on the car were all closed.

"Okay, since you can 'talk', tell me, what did I have for breakfast yesterday?" I asked.

"A cream filled chocolate doughnut and a cup of coffee," Gracie answered.

Lucky guess. Let's try again.

"Alright, Ms. Know-it-all. Where did we go last weekend?"

"To Munsen's Nature Reserve. We hiked, stopped by the waterfall for lunch. You let me play in the stream."

Either I had a stalker or....nope, don't want to go into the realm of impossibility.

"One more question."

"Beth…"

"Gracie. What was I wearing the day I adopted you and where were you when you were adopted?"

Gracie rolled her eyes and sighed.

"You came into Fast Gas pulling a U-Haul trailer behind your car. You had on black denim jeans and a blue short sleeved shirt with lace around the neck. You walked out with a bottle of water, and you saw a lady standing there holding me. She told you I was the last of my litter." Oh. My. God! My dog talks. *TALKS!*

"Let's pretend I believe you can talk. Tell me, why haven't you said anything to me before now?"

"I haven't been able to. The magic in this town enables me to be my true self. This is where I was born many years ago. To you, I'm only a year old, but I'm actually hundreds of years old."

"That's not possible! When I got you, you were just a puppy!"

"I remained in puppy form until I found my human. I was destined to be chosen by you. The old woman you got me from is a witch."

"Whoa. Okay hold on. A witch. Uh-huh. Yeah. What is in this water bottle? Not drinking any more of this."

"Honest Beth. We were destined to be together."

"Alright. Say I believe in talking dogs, witches, destiny and all that. What exactly am I supposed to do with this information?"

"This is our town. It's a magical town where we belong."

"Our town? Uh huh. Okay. And, why, pray tell, is it 'our' town?"

"This is where we are destined to be. Do you think it's a coincidence the witch just appeared in the gas station parking lot right as you came out? She saw you in a vision and predicted that you and I were meant to be together in this town. You need to call Anna and go look at that house I pointed out. That house is where the next chapter of our destiny begins."

I turned back around in my seat, fastened my seat belt, started the car and prepared to drive home. "Let me think about this."

"As you wish but know this, once we leave the boundaries of the town, I won't be able to human-speak anymore. Only here can we communicate."

"I understand. Home, we go."

*****

The man stepped out from the side of the realty company and watched as Beth drove off. He retrieved his cell phone from his jacket pocket and placed a call.

"Hey! I wanted to let you know about a woman who was just here. She was with a talking dog. I'm not sure who or what she is but we need to watch her. She could be trouble." Then he disconnected the call.

Chapter Three

I woke up the next morning convinced the previous day was all a dream. Talking dogs and magical towns. Right!

I noticed Gracie wasn't in the bedroom with me, which was unusual. I got up and headed for the kitchen where Gracie was lying on her dog bed.

"Good morning, my girl. You're up early."

I grabbed a mug out of the cabinet and poured a cup of coffee.

"Ready for some breakfast?"

Gracie looked at me but didn't move from her bed.

"Okay then."

I got her breakfast ready then grabbed a cinnamon raisin bagel for myself. When I sat down at the counter, Gracie got up from her bed and walked over to me. I noticed she had a piece of paper in her mouth.

"What do you have there, girl? Let's see."

I took the paper from her just as I took a sip of coffee. When I saw the paper Gracie brought to me, I spit coffee all over the counter. It was the listing for the house in the town we were in yesterday.

I jumped up, dropping the listing on the counter. I grabbed some paper towels to clean up the mess.

"Where did you get this?" I asked while furiously swiping the paper towels through the mess.

Gracie looked at me and placed her paw on my foot.

"Oh my god, oh my god, oh my god! It wasn't a dream." I started hyperventilating.

Talking dogs! Witches! Magical towns! My dog with a real estate listing that I know I didn't pick up. What is happening to me? I must be getting sick. Yes, that's it. I have delirium caused by a high fever from a virus I've picked up.

I felt my forehead and my cheeks, then went to get a thermometer from the bathroom. My temperature was normal.

I knocked the paper off the counter. Gracie pawed my foot.

"Ok Beth, breathe. Just breathe. In, out. Breathe," I said, trying to calm myself.

I flopped back down in my chair.

Have I mentioned lately that I might benefit from therapy? I'm becoming more and more convinced of that with every day that goes by.

Gracie picked up the paper in her mouth and shoved her nose toward me repeatedly until I took the paper again.

When I had finally gotten control of myself and was sure I wasn't going to keel over, I smoothed the paper out, now wrinkled and wet with dog slobber and coffee, and looked at the listing. It *is* a really nice house and it's priced affordably.

Wait, what am I thinking? But it is nice and would be great to actually have a house. I could have a home office instead of a desk in the kitchen. Since I ran my business from home, it wouldn't be a problem moving it. I communicated with my clients by email, phone, and fax, so that wouldn't be an issue either as long as I had internet service. Gracie could have a yard. The house didn't need that much work, just a few cosmetic and personal touches.

"Alright Gracie. I'll call Anna and ask about the house. No promises though, deal?"

Gracie wagged her tail and barked her agreement.

I dug the card out of my purse, picked up my cell phone and called the number of Full Moon Realty printed on the card Anna had given me yesterday.

"Full Moon Realty. Anna speaking. How can I help make your dreams come true?"

"Hi Anna. This is Beth Woodson. We met yesterday at the dog park?"

"Dog park? Oh yes, the park! Beth! Hi! How are you?"

"Fine thanks! Listen, somehow, I must have picked up a flyer for a house that you have listed, and I'd like some information on it."

I wasn't about to tell her my talking dog grabbed the listing because she decided we had to buy a house there. It would probably be the shortest conversation in history.

"Oh yes. The house on Wagon Pass?"

"Uh, yes. How did you…"

"Perfect! If you have time, I could show it to you today. It really is a darling house. I think it would be a perfect fit for you."

"S-s-sure. Uh. I can be there in an hour."

"Great! I'll see you then!"

I hung up and looked at Gracie's eager face.

"Okay Gracie. We're going to see the house. Just let me shower really quick."

Gracie woofed her agreement, wagged her tail, and began eating her breakfast.

After showering, I loaded Gracie into the car, and we set out to see the house. Today the sun was shining brightly. Big white fluffy clouds hung in the sky and flowers in a multitude of colors and varieties were blooming and seemed to have popped up everywhere overnight. It was a perfect day. Then my phone rang. *Asshat* showed on the display. Well, the day was *almost* perfect. I hit ignore.

Gracie and I arrived in town, and I parked in front of Anna's realty company. We exited the car and entered the office. Anna was on the phone and waved at me.

I sat in one of the plush chairs in the waiting area as Anna finished up her call. I looked around at the beautiful artwork hanging on the walls around the office. It appeared they were all hand-painted pictures of different areas around town.

On one wall was a board with realty listings tacked to it. Maybe it was my imagination, but one listing in particular seemed to glow. I got up from my chair to get a closer look. It was the house that we were preparing to look at.

I couldn't take my eyes off it as all these thoughts and plans started swirling through my head. Decorating plans, paint colors. I shook my head to clear the thoughts and to stop myself from getting carried away. I hadn't even seen the place yet, but I was already planning. For all I knew right now, it was a falling down shack and the pictures had been computer generated.

Anna walked over to us and smiled.

"Beth! So glad you could come today. This house is a real gem. Just needs the right person to love it. Are you ready to see it?"

"Yes, let's."

Gracie and I walked with Anna out to her SUV.

"We'll take my car if that's okay with you."

"Is it okay for Gracie to ride? If not, I can take my car."

"No, she's more than welcome to ride. You forget, I have children."

Gracie hopped in the backseat. I shut the door and climbed into the front, fastening my seatbelt. Anna's SUV was immaculate except for bits of dog hair here and there.

"Do you have a dog too?" I asked.

Anna looked at me with a puzzled look on her face.

"No, although Daisy has been begging her father and me for one. Why do you ask?"

What should I say? Uhhh....

"Oh no reason. I thought Daisy mentioned something about it yesterday and she seemed so good with Gracie." Nice save, Beth!

"Nope. No dogs. Just the two kids."

I thought maybe the dog hair had come from another client's dog. After all, she didn't seem to have a problem with Gracie riding in here. That had to be it!

"You are really going to love this house, Beth. It's just so.... you."

We drove about 10 minutes out of town and Anna turned down a nicely landscaped residential street. A short distance up, the house came into view. It sat on a cul-de-sac and the three other houses there looked to be neat and very well maintained. So far, so good. The houses were spaced a comfortable distance apart to allow each resident privacy.

The one I was looking at was a cute one-story ranch home. A covered porch wrapped around from the front, disappearing around the sides. There was a driveway in the front of the house with an offshoot that went around to the back. White columns graced the porch and a beautiful solid oak door with decorative glass beckoned us to enter.

I got out of Anna's car and opened the door for Gracie. She ran off to investigate the yard. Anna and I climbed three steps up to the front porch. Anna put a code into a box attached to the doorknob and a compartment popped open that held a key. She placed it in the door lock, turned the doorknob and opened the front door.

"Now, let me see," Anna said looking at a paper in her hand.

"The house has three bedrooms, two and a half baths. There's a fireplace not only here in the living room but also in the master bedroom and they are both functioning wood burning fireplaces. The flues were just recently inspected and passed. The fireplaces are great for those chilly autumn nights when you don't really want to run the heater."

"There's a large gourmet kitchen, situated so that it catches the morning sun. All appliances are top of the line, and they stay with the house. The bathrooms have been updated and the master has a jacuzzi tub with a separate shower. The furnace, A/C, and water heater have all been replaced too. New flooring throughout."

"There's a smaller room that can be used as an office, library, whatever you see fit to use it for. There is also a pull-down staircase that grants access to the attic for additional storage. The roof, although it looks like shingles, is metal and comes with a transferable lifetime warranty. The house was recently insulated with R-30 rated insulation. The basement is unfinished but offers up a lot of potential."

"The property is approximately two acres, one cleared around the house, the rest in woods. I have the number of a lawn care service if that's something you think you'd be interested in. The house itself is a bit over 2,000 square feet. Feel free to wander around and check it all out. If you have any other questions, let me know."

I walked around looking at everything. The living room had a bay window, complete with a built-in window seat that looked out over the front yard. Built-in bookcases flanked the fireplace. I could see myself curled up on my sofa in front of a fire, drinking a cup of tea and reading.

I checked out the kitchen and was amazed at the size. The appliances gleamed in the morning sun, just begging to be used. A triple sink with a disposal sat on an island along with a Jenn-Aire cook top. Built-in ovens, both conventional and convection, were behind the island. An oversized double-door refrigerator and a sub-zero freezer sat next to the ovens. The tile backsplash was gorgeous and complimented the gleaming granite counters. There was even a wine refrigerator! A breakfast nook was on the opposite side in front of large windows that looked out into the yard. A walk-through butler's pantry was just off the kitchen, leading out to the hallway. The bedrooms were on both sides of the hall.

The master bedroom was much bigger than I ever imagined. A beautiful stone mantle graced the fireplace. Another bay window overlooked the woods behind the house. There was an oversized walk-in closet as well. The master bath off the bedroom was stylishly appointed with the most modern fixtures and, oh, that tub! Gorgeous! I could see myself lighting candles and soaking in a bubble bath. The detached shower had a stone surround and was large enough for two to fit comfortably. Not that I had to worry about that!

Next, I checked out the remaining two bedrooms, both good sized with a hall bathroom separating them. The attic access was in the hall ceiling. I could see the access and the cord hanging for the drop-down steps but didn't bother with it. The half bath was situated at the end of the hall next to the smaller bonus room Anna had mentioned. It would make a great home office. The hall ended back into the living room.

Anna was checking her phone when I walked back over to where she was standing.

"So, what do you think? Gorgeous, right?"

"Anna, I love it. But before I make an offer, I need to know what's wrong with it? So much work has been done, but the price...."

"Well, I'll be honest with you Beth. The previous owner worked remotely for a big accounting firm. Actually, she was the one who did the accounting for most of the businesses in town, in addition to her regular job. She was up for a big promotion and when she got it, she moved to be closer to her work. A commute from here wasn't feasible now that she no longer worked remotely."

"Plus, she'd always said the house didn't feel like 'home' to her, regardless of how much work she did to it. She never really elaborated on why she felt that way, just said she wasn't a good fit for the property. When the promotion came through, she jumped at it. The property has sat empty for a year or so, but it's been waiting for the right person to come in and take it over. I feel it in my bones, YOU are the right person."

I thought it over for a few minutes, then said, "Ok, let's go make an offer."

Anna clapped her hands together and said, "Marvelous! I just knew you would love this place!"

We went back outside, and I whistled for Gracie. Anna stopped what she was doing and looked at me strangely. She shook her head and continued locking up the house. Gracie came bounding towards me, tongue hanging out, tail in the air, and if a dog could smile, I'd swear that's what she was doing.

We went back to Anna's office and wrote up a contract. Within minutes of Anna faxing over my offer, her phone rang.

She looked at her phone and said, "Excuse me a moment. It's the seller."

She spoke on the phone for a few minutes then said, "Wonderful! I'll let her know! Thank you so much Susie! Hope the new job is going well. Give my love to your mother. Take care now!" She disconnected and looked at me smiling.

"Good news! The seller has accepted your offer!"

"Wow! That was quick!"

"Yes, but when it's right, it just is! Welcome to Raven's Glen, Beth! You're going to love it here! And, with you being an accountant, you will be a much-welcomed addition to the town."

We finalized a few more details, Anna hugged me goodbye, then I loaded up Gracie to go back to our apartment to start the financing process. Wow! I couldn't believe it! I was about to be a homeowner!

*****

A man was standing on the sidewalk a few doors down from the realty company. When Beth came out talking to Anna about purchasing and getting financed for the house, the man walked a little way down the sidewalk. When he was sure he wouldn't be overheard, he took his phone out and placed a call.

"Apparently the woman that was here yesterday has now purchased a home here."

He listened, then said, "I agree. We will keep an eye on her."

And then he disconnected.

Chapter Four

Moving day came quickly. Earlier in the week I'd reserved a moving truck from McGoogle's (like I said before, they sold everything) and the last of my belongings were being loaded, not that I had a lot to begin with. Anna graciously sent her brother-in-law and his friend to help me move.

They picked up the truck from McGoogle's and drove to my apartment. We would finish loading the truck, then they'd drive the rental to the house, and I'd follow in my car. When we were done, they would also return the truck. I offered them payment, but they'd declined, saying any friend of Anna's was a friend of theirs.

"Here we go, Gracie. Onward to our new adventure!" Gracie barked in agreement.

We arrived at the house in no time. Anna and Daisy were parked in the driveway waiting for us. I pulled in behind the moving truck, got out of the car at the same time Anna and Daisy got out of the SUV, and opened the back door to let Gracie out. I walked up to where Anna and Daisy were standing. Gracie ran straight to Daisy. The two of them walked over to sit on the porch and started talking like they were old friends.

I looked nervously at Anna to see if she noticed my dog was talking. It didn't appear she did.

"Welcome to your new home, Beth," Anna said smiling.

She was holding a large, divided basket with a bow on top. She handed me the basket and said, "A little moving day gift."

On one side were jars of jam, freshly baked bread, scones, and muffins, and a small bottle of wine. The other side had candles, soaps, and lotions. An envelope containing gift certificates for businesses in town was lying on top. There were even dog treats for Gracie!

"This is so sweet! But you didn't have to do this, Anna," I said as I continued checking out the contents.

"We just wanted to do a little something special to welcome you. All of the items in there are locally crafted. A lot of people from here contributed. They're all excited to meet you, Beth." Anna pulled me in for a hug.

I was overwhelmed. I'd never lived anywhere where I was instantly accepted and welcomed.

"Well, thank you so much, Anna."

Anna called over her shoulder to Daisy who was still sitting on the front porch with Gracie.

"Anyway, Daisy and I will let you start getting settled in. Again, Welcome, Beth! If you need anything at all, don't hesitate to call me."

Daisy hugged Gracie then walked down to Anna and me. She threw her tiny arms around my legs, hugging me.

"I'm so glad you and Gracie moved here, Ms. Beth."

The guys got the truck unpacked and set up the limited amount of furniture I had where I'd showed them. Gracie was out exploring her new surroundings. When they left to take the truck back to McGoogle's, I called for Gracie, then I started unpacking some of the boxes—just the essentials tonight. I planned to dive in earnestly tomorrow.

I unpacked a few towels, wash cloths, and toiletry items and put them in the master bathroom. A nice long soak in that Jacuzzi tub was on the agenda.

I found the sheets, pillows and pillowcases, and a comforter and made up my bed. I unpacked a few kitchen items, mainly the coffee maker, coffee, and a mug, and set that up in the kitchen.

Wow! This was really mine!

After unpacking a few more essentials, I went into the bathroom and turned on the faucets to fill the jacuzzi tub. I put a few drops of bubble bath in, went to the bedroom for fresh undergarments and pajamas and waited as the tub filled with warm water. I'd brought in one of the candles that was in the basket Anna had given me and lit it. It soon filled the bathroom with the relaxing scent of lavender and vanilla. Gracie was napping on her dog bed in my bedroom, worn out from all the fresh air today as she explored her new yard.

I turned off the taps, set the timer on the jets, and hung my robe on the wall hook next to the tub. I sank into the delicious and relaxing warmth and turned the jets on low. Ahhh! Home sweet home!

The warmth relaxed me so much, I must have dozed off. The water was now lukewarm, and the jets had shut off. I was startled awake by Gracie having a conversation with someone in the bedroom. I wasn't expecting company so I wasn't sure who could possibly be out there and how they got inside. I knew I'd locked the doors after I let Gracie in earlier.

I sat up and peeked around the side of the tub. I couldn't see outside of the bathroom since the door was half closed. I stood up, got out of the tub, toweled off quickly, then grabbed my robe off the hook on the wall next to the tub. I walked to the door and peeked out. I saw Gracie sitting up on her dog bed looking toward the corner. She would listen for a few minutes, then respond to an unseen visitor. She didn't seem alarmed, so I opened the bathroom door all the way and stepped into the bedroom.

"Gracie? Who are you talking to?"

Suddenly I heard a scream coming from somewhere in the bedroom. Have you ever seen the cartoon where the startled cat jumps up and is hanging upside down from the ceiling by his claws? That's how I felt right now.

"Gracie! Who were you talking to and who screamed? Was it you? Please tell me it was you!"

I didn't want to think about or imagine the alternative.

"It wasn't me, Beth. It was Bart. He lives here. I'm afraid you scared him," Gracie answered in the most nonchalant way possible.

"What in Hell's crackerjacks box are you talking about? No one named Bart lives here."

"Yes, Beth, he does. Give me a second and I'll see if I can get him to come back, then I will introduce you."

"Gracie, you're scaring me right now. Why is a strange man living in our house?"

Maybe I *should* have checked out the attic before buying the house!

"Calm down, Beth. I'll explain when I can get Bart to come back."

To the empty room, Gracie said, "Come back Bart. I want you to meet Beth."

I saw a glow appear in the corner of the bedroom.

"Uhhhh, Gracie."

"Remain calm, Beth. Come on Bart. It's okay."

The glowing light got a little brighter.

Gracie looked at me and said, "Beth, this is Bart. Bart, this is my human Beth. We just moved in."

Confused now by an introduction to someone I couldn't see, I started looking around the room which was lit up by the gorgeous full moon shining through the window. I saw a man standing in the corner next to the bay window surrounded by a pale blue glow. I screamed, he screamed, then disappeared.

Gracie raced over to my side, as I stood wide-eyed and gasping for air.

"What the...who...I..."

"Beth, calm down. What's wrong?"

"Gracie Eliza Woodson! What just happened? How did that man get inside my house? Who is he and where did he go?"

"Beth, calm down. Let me explain. The man you saw was Bart. He's a ghost. He built this house in 1899 for his soon-to-be bride. Unfortunately, she was killed when the buggy that was bringing her to the wedding overturned on the way. Bart was so distraught that he lived here the rest of his life alone. He still lives here, as it is, waiting for the ghost of his beloved fiancé. He can't move on until they are reunited."

"What?!? A ghost? Here? In this house?"

"Yes, Beth, a ghost. I told you this was a magical town. But I'm afraid you've scared him. He spooks easily, no pun intended."

"*I* scared *him*? Really, Gracie?"

"Yes, now hang on. I'm going to see if I can get him to come back."

"Oh no! We are NOT living in a haunted house. No wonder it was so cheap. I'm calling Anna first thing tomorrow and we're moving. We're going back to our apartment. Hopefully Greg hasn't rented it out yet. No way! Not staying! No way, no how! Best of luck to you, Mr. Ghost. You can have your house back. We'll be leaving first thing tomorrow."

"Beth, stop being silly. The house isn't haunted. Bart is honestly more scared of you than you are of him. Trust me. Just talk to him. You'll see he's a great guy!"

"Great GUY?? He's a GHOST Gracie! There's no 'guy' involved!"

Gracie ignored my rambling and called out for Bart.

"Come on Bart. Beth didn't mean to scare you. All of this is new to her. It's my fault really. I should have explained your presence a little better. If she promises not to scream again, will you please come back?"

A disembodied voice answered. "Do you promise she won't scream again? It scared me so bad!"

"I promise! Beth, promise please."

"I, uh, I promise I will try not to scream."

"Okay."

A transparent head appeared in the corner. I sucked in a breath and the head started to disappear.

"Beth, you promised," Gracie admonished me.

"I know. I'm fine, really."

The head started materializing again. It was followed by a neck and a set of shoulders.

"Come on now Bart. It's okay. Just a little bit more."

Bart's chest, stomach then legs appeared. He seemed to be trembling and now surrounded by a yellow glow. He was tall and lanky and was dressed in a three-piece old timey suit. A pocket watch chain hung from a pocket on the vest. He was holding a formal hat in his hands.

"See, it's all good. Beth, once again, this is Bart. Bart, Beth."

Bart wouldn't look at me, instead looking at his feet, which had just reappeared. "Good evening, Miss Beth. S-s-s-sorry I s-s-s-scared you."

"Oh, no. Apologies are mine. I just wasn't expecting to see you," I responded, clearly either in the throes of a really strange dream or insanity. I'm thinking the latter. Maybe it was too late for therapy. Maybe I should just go straight to the nice white padded room.

Still not looking at me, Bart continued. "Sorry about the mess I made on the floor here. I have a nervous bowel."

I looked to where Bart stood and noticed what looked like a pile of M&Ms on the floor.

"Is that......uhhh?"

"Yes, and I'm so sorry. It usually happens when I get scared. Or nervous. Hungry. Happy. Anyway, sorry. But don't worry, it will disappear in a bit."

Sure enough, the pile disappeared.

"Uh, thanks Bart?"

"So, Beth, as Bart and I were discussing prior to your appearance, he'd like to find his fiancé. I told him perhaps you could help him find her. It's really a tragic love story and after all these years, Bart deserves to have a little happiness. Loralee was his one true love and he hers. What do you think?"

"Ouch!" I cried out as I pinched myself on the arm.

I was awake so yes; I'd lost my mind.

Bart disappeared again, another pile of M&Ms appearing in the corner. Geez!

"Bart, I'm sorry. I didn't mean to scare you. Please come back." A hat appeared, but nothing else.

"Y-y-you s-s-scared me again. P-p-please stop."

"Again, I'm so sorry Bart. Really. This is all new to me. I've had a lot of new things I've had to learn to deal with lately, so excuse me while I try to get accustomed to you and this situation. Please come back so we can talk about how I can help you."

Bart appeared a little quicker than before.

"Okay, but please, no loud voices. My nerves just can't take it."

His nerves? Yeah. Like my nerves were doing so much better as evidenced by the way my heart was pounding and my insides felt like a big bowl of jello. I guess talking to imaginary people will do that to a person.

"Scouts honor. Is it okay if I go in and get dressed? I'm getting a little chilly standing here in my robe. Then we can sit down and talk."

"S-s-sure. Please do. I'm sorry."

"It's fine Bart. Just excuse me for one second."

I returned to the bathroom to put my pajamas on, all the while wondering what was happening to me. First my dog talks. Talks! Now I have a ghost living in my house. What's next? Flying monkeys? I shuddered at that thought. Of course I'm getting to the point I don't think much would surprise me anymore. I'll just sit in the corner, babbling to myself, watching the flying monkeys while playing poker with a ghost and my talking dog.

If was then, realizing Bart was a ghost and could appear anywhere, I wondered if he could see me dressing. This caused me to speed up the process. I put my robe on again over my pajamas and went out to the bedroom. As soon as I stepped over the threshold into the bedroom, Bart screamed and disappeared yet again.

"Oh, for the love of Pete. Bart! It's me. Stop popping in and out. You're freaking me out!"

"Please don't yell at me," Bart whined.

"Just come on out and let's talk."

I walked over to the bed and sat just as Bart hesitantly reappeared.

I decided to just roll with this crazy fantasy, or dream, or bout with blatant insanity. Why not? Let's just jump right on the crazy train and see where it takes us! Wheeee! Hang on, folks! Down the rabbit hole we go!

"So, Bart. What can I do to help you? I've never dealt with something like this, and I don't know how much help I will be."

"Well, Miss Beth. My beloved Loralee, as you've heard, was on her way here so that we could be married. She was a tiny little thing, gorgeous blonde hair, eyes so blue you could swim in forever. Soft-spoken, gentle, always so pleasant. She was the prettiest girl in all of Missouri and I was surprised when she showed interest in me. I mean, I'm, well, it's just, I'm not exactly...." His prominent Adam's apple bobbed up and down as he nervously gulped.

"I get it, Bart. Please continue."

"I was just so honored that this beautiful woman was not only interested in me but agreed to be my wife! I had this house built especially for her. She deserved the best and money was no object."

"May I ask a question, Bart? She wasn't marrying you for money, was she? And are you sure she, uh, was really in a buggy accident and didn't just get cold feet and back out?"

"Oh no, Miss Beth. You see, Loralee's family was quite well off. She certainly didn't need my money. Plus, I had to help the men remove her from the wreckage. It was the hardest thing I have ever had to do, besides bury her, that is."

"I see. Please go on."

"So, I'm here, waiting for my one true love to arrive. The house was all decorated, guests were starting to arrive. The preacher was bringing her. Well, it started getting late and I started getting nervous, thinking she'd changed her mind. I visited the outhouse several times. Nervous bowel, like I said. On one of my trips back in from the outhouse, little Jaime Norris came running up to me. Told me there'd been an accident just down the road. Said some of the neighbors came upon it when they were on the way here."

Bart had his hat in his hands, worrying the brim of it round and round as he relived that horrible day. The glow around him turned a deep blue.

"Jaime and I took off down the road and when I saw the overturned buggy, I panicked. I knew that buggy belonged to the preacher. A bunch of the menfolk from town were already there. As I was helping the men trying to right the buggy, I caught a glimpse of an ivory dress, and I fell to pieces right there. The other men finally got the buggy righted, but Loralee and the preacher had been pinned beneath the wreckage. My world ended that day, Miss Beth. I returned home but was too distraught to tell the guests what had happened. I went straight to my room and laid on the bed. I stayed there for several days until someone came to fetch me and escort me to the funeral. Afterwards, I came back here and never left the house again."

I noticed my face was wet from the tears that had started during his heartbreaking story, all traces of my earlier skepticism gone. How awful to love someone that deeply, only to lose them before you can even start your lives together.

"I lived on another 50 years. Every day without Loralee was hell. Excuse me, ma'am—heck. When my final day on this earth came, my spirit couldn't just up and leave. I must find my Loralee. Then we can go to the Pearly Gates and spend our eternity together. Something we were robbed of in life."

"Bart, I am so sorry for your loss! I can't imagine the depth of the pain you've felt all these years. How about this? Tomorrow, you can show me where the accident happened, if you think you're up to it, and we'll see what we can find out. I can't make any promises, but it's a start."

"Oh, Miss Beth. That is so kind of you. I haven't been back to that spot since that dreadful day, but the location is etched into my soul. I stayed here in case Loralee came looking for me. I was afraid if I left, even for one second, Loralee would come, and I'd miss her. Never happened though."

"But, Bart, we need to set up some ground rules while you're here."

"Anything, Miss Beth."

"Okay, first don't just suddenly pop up in front of me or it may be me joining you in the spirit world. Announce yourself somehow before just appearing."

"Yes ma'am. I can do that."

"Second, no watching me while I'm sleeping. Or bathing. Dressing. None of those. Understand? A girl needs her privacy."

If it was possible for a ghost to blush, I think Bart would have been since the glowing light around him turned bright pink.

He looked at his feet, worrying the brim of his hat again.

"Oh, no ma'am. I'm a gentleman. I could never do such...." His Adam's apple bobbed up and down again.

"It's alright, Bart. Now, if you'll excuse me, I am worn out from all the moving today and I really need to get some sleep."

"Yes ma'am. And, again, thank you so much! Goodnight."

He put his hat back on his head, touched the brim of it with his fingers, tipping it a bit, and with that, Bart disappeared.

I stood and took off my robe, laying it across the foot of the bed, then pulled back the covers. I climbed into bed and got comfortable. I heard Gracie settling into her dog bed.

"Beth?" Gracie asked. "Do you think we can find out something about Loralee and what happened to her? Bart is such a nice guy, and he deserves to be happy."

"I'm not sure, Gracie, especially considering how many years have passed since the accident. I'm not even sure how to go about finding a ghost but I thought going back to where she died might be a good start.

Bart said he hadn't been back there since the accident. Maybe Loralee is hanging around there. It's a start at least. Let's get some rest and see what we find tomorrow. Goodnight, my girl."

"Goodnight, Beth. Thanks for moving here. It's going to be great!"

Sure it was. As long as I didn't wind up having a massive heart attack! Or getting carted off by the nice men in white coats. And I thought the only thing I had to worry about was Grams and her shenanigans. Ha!

Chapter Five

The next morning, I got up out of bed, slipped on my robe and house shoes and padded into the kitchen. I poured that heavenly first cup of coffee and got a blueberry scone from the gift basket, then sat at the breakfast nook. The sun was just coming up and lit the kitchen with a warm glow.

I had some quarterly tax returns to do today for some of my customers once I'd gotten my computer hooked up, but those wouldn't take long. Besides, I promised Bart I'd help him. I think. Maybe I'd just dreamed the whole thing.

"Beth, Bart would like to know if he can appear. He didn't want to startle you, as per your agreement."

"Sure, Gracie, tell him he's more than welcome."

That put to rest the dream theory.

Bart slowly appeared by the kitchen island. He was surrounded by a rosy-colored glow today.

"Good morning, Miss Beth. Thank you for allowing me to appear. Whenever you're ready, I can take you to the site where I lost my Loralee."

"Sure Bart. Let me get dressed and we'll go."

"Splendid, Miss Beth. Just call out to me when you're ready." And with that, Bart popped out.

I finished my coffee and scone, then rinsed my mug in the sink. I went into my bedroom and grabbed a pair of jeans, a T-shirt, socks and tennis shoes and went into the bathroom to get dressed. I brushed my teeth, then my long brown hair and put it up in a ponytail.

When I was ready, I went back to the kitchen and called out to Bart. He reappeared by the back door. I grabbed my house keys and phone and put them in a small backpack with a few bottles of water. I added a handful of dog biscuits for Gracie as well. I wasn't sure how far we were going but wanted some supplies.

Bart floated through the back door. I was going to test that dream theory one last time and started to follow Bart through the door. When I bounced off the solid object and ended up on the floor on my backside, Gracie looked at me.

"Beth?"

"Sorry, Gracie. Just checking something out."

"And that would be what? Theories on solid matter and concussions?"

"Never mind!"

I opened the door for Gracie and me to go out. I didn't bother with a leash, figuring I'd let Gracie explore her new surroundings some more. I locked the door behind us, and we set off towards the woods.

"I can't tell you how much I appreciate your help, Miss Beth. I've never been brave enough to revisit the site but with you and Gracie, I think I'll be okay."

"Awww, Bart. It's no problem! There's no guarantee we'll find anything, so try not to get your hopes up. It's a start at least. So how far is it to the site?"

"It's not too far away. We follow this trail, and it leads down to a creek. The accident happened just across the creek and around the bend."

"Can we cross the creek on foot?"

"Oh yes ma'am. It's a wet weather creek. Only gets up after rain."

We walked along the trail in the woods behind my house and chatted about everyday things as we went. Gracie had raced ahead exploring the wildlife and sniffing every leaf, tree, and blade of grass she came upon.

"Bart, if I may ask a question, what is the glowing ring around you that changes colors?"

"It's sort of like an aura, but it changes color, depending on how I feel."

"I see. So, it's sort of like a spectral mood ring?"

I couldn't tamp down the giggle that was trying to escape.

"I'm sorry, Bart. I'm not making fun of you."

"Oh no, Miss Beth. It is sort of like a mood ring," Bart chuckled.

Soon we came to a dip in the trail which led to the now dry creek bed.

"It's just up here around the bend. Not much farther."

As soon as we crossed the creek, the trail turned to the right. Once it straightened out, we came to a small clearing. There was a large rock sticking up from the ground in the middle of the trail.

"Has that rock always been here Bart?"

"Yes ma'am. Used to be just a tiny bit of the top stuck up. We always tried to miss it when we brought the buggies through here. Over the years erosion started exposing just how big a rock it is, but it wasn't like that back then. If you didn't know it was there and you hit it, it could damage your buggy wheels or cause the horse to get a lame foot. Anyway, we think the buggy hit the rock and that's why it overturned."

Bart and I searched around the trail and surrounding woods finding nothing. Bart called out to Loralee a few times, but nothing seemed to be working.

"I think it's no use Miss Beth. I think my Loralee must have moved on without me."

Bart's glow started turning a dark blue.

"I am so sorry Bart. But I promise you I won't give up. We'll keep looking."

"Thanks Miss Beth. I think I'm going to pop out and rest for a while."

I turned around and started heading back towards my house. After I crossed the creek, I saw an older gentleman walking toward me. He was dressed in a pair of jeans and a short sleeved button up shirt. He had a bottle of water in one hand and a walking stick in the other. When he got closer, he smiled and greeted me. His gray eyes were kind and crinkled in the corners when he smiled.

Gracie stopped next to him, greeting him with a spoken "Good morning!" and he stooped to pet her. She then raced around him a few times before shooting off ahead.

I waited nervously for the man's reaction to a talking dog, but he seemed to act like dogs speaking to him were just a normal part of his day.

"Hello Miss! Beautiful day for a wilderness walk,

heh?" I noticed he spoke with a slight accent.

Normally I'd be a bit cautious about talking to strangers I came across while walking in the woods. But Gracie seemed to have had no problem with him when she met him, and she was close enough to help if something happened.

"Good morning. Yes, it is a beautiful day."

I wasn't about to tell him I'd followed a ghost out here to search for his likewise ghostly fiancé. That would be a quick way to be escorted right out of town. A talking dog was one thing. Maybe I was the only one who could hear her talk. Maybe others only heard a bark. I wasn't going to push it.

"Are you new to these parts? I can't recall ever meeting you before."

"Yes. I'm Beth Woodson. My dog Gracie is the fur blur that raced past you a few seconds ago. We just moved here."

"Pleasure to meet you Ms. Woodson. I'm Giuseppe Romano. I believe we are neighbors. I have the house behind yours just over the hill. Would you mind if I walked with you a bit? I normally come out here to walk every morning and it isn't often I get to have the company of such a lovely young lady."

"Thank you, Mr. Romano, and please call me Beth."

"Very well, Beth. And you may call me Giuseppe. So how are you enjoying our little town? Finding everything you need okay?"

"I haven't really had much time to explore. Gracie and I just moved in yesterday. I've been busy unpacking and getting the house set up."

"I see. What do you do for work, Ms…ah, Beth?"

"I run an accounting business from my home."

"Oh splendid! Splendid! I own Giuseppe's Italian Restaurant here in town and I may be in the market for a new accountant. My former one moved away and my beautiful wife Francesca has been tending to the books. She's none too happy to be stuck in the office instead of out mingling with the guests."

"I'd be more than happy to talk to you about it."

"Well please come to Guiseppe's as my guest. Sort of a welcome to the town gift. You can have a nice lunch and afterwards, we can talk business. Mondays are best since we are closed that day. This way, you'll experience all the greatness of Giuseppe's without the hustle and bustle of a normal business day. And it will be much easier to talk."

"That's very generous. Thank you so much Guiseppe."

"No problem, Beth. We're a very close community here and like to welcome our newcomers with open arms and full bellies!" Giuseppe laughed and I joined in.

We walked a bit further, chatting about the town, and then Giuseppe said, "Well Beth, this is where I must take my leave. It's been a pleasure walking and talking with you. Benvenuta! Welcome! And please stop by a week from today at, shall we say, 11 a.m.? I fix you a nice meal."

"I will and thank you!"

Giuseppe turned to the left and headed in the opposite direction from my house. Gracie was waiting for me on the back porch when I got there.

"I just met one of the neighbors, Gracie. He seemed very nice and is interested in speaking to me about taking over his accounting."

"That's terrific! But I feel so bad for Bart. I was really hoping we'd be able to help him."

"I know what you mean, girl, but we won't give up. I'll keep searching for Loralee."

Once Beth was out of earshot Giuseppe took his cell phone out and made a call.

"It's me. I was out on my daily patrol of the woods and just had the pleasure of speaking with our newest resident. I've invited her to the restaurant as my guest."

He listened for a few seconds and then said, "She seems very nice and cordial, but I agree, we need to continue to watch her for the time being. When I mentioned her being in the woods, she said she was just out walking, but I get the feeling she was hiding something."

Neither Giuseppe nor Beth saw the figure hiding in the woods watching them.

Chapter Six

When Gracie and I got back to the house, I started unpacking and setting up my office. As I was hooking up the last cable on my computer, my phone rang. *Mom* showed on the display.

"Hi Mom."

"Hi honey. How's the move going? Getting unpacked and settled in?"

"Yep. I'm working on setting up my office now so I can get a couple of client quarterlies done. What's going on down your way? How's Dad?"

"Oh, you know your dad. Since he retired, he spends a lot of time on the golf course. But better on their green than in my gray—hair, that is"

I chuckled. Mom and Dad were just as much in love today as they were when they met in high school. I hoped one day to have the type of relationship they had. As soon as my dad retired, they sold their house and moved to Florida to be closer to my grandmother. It didn't hurt that their new house was in a subdivision with its own golf course.

"Is Jason still bothering you?"

"Oh yeah. He calls me at least three or four times a week. He just won't give up."

"He knows he lost a good thing when you left. He sure fooled all of us. But hang in there sweetie. You'll meet the right one."

"I know, Mom. Right now I'm more interested in getting settled into my new house."

"Listen, have you heard from your grandmother lately? I've called her several times, but her phone always goes to voicemail. I'm guessing she's gotten up to something and is avoiding my calls."

"Come to think of it, no. I haven't heard from her in a while."

"Would you mind trying to get a hold of her? She always answers when you call. Make sure she's not hurt or sick. Or in jail." I could just see my mother rolling her eyes.

"Sure, Mom. I'll give her a call as soon as I finish getting my computer hooked up."

"Thanks sweetie. Let us know once you get settled. Your dad and I would love to come visit and see the new house. And if you have a golf course there, you probably won't even realize your dad is there." Mom chuckled.

"Will do, Mom. Love you. Tell Dad I love him too."

"I will, sweetheart. Love you. Take care."

I hung up with my mother, finished hooking up my computer and turned it on. Anna had arranged to get the internet and Wi-Fi installed before I moved in, along with making sure the utilities were on. While I was waiting for my computer to boot up, I dialed my grandmother. She answered on the second ring.

"Hello Bethie Lynn. How's the new house?"

It was quiet in the background, so maybe that was a good sign she was behaving herself.

"Oh, Grams, it's beautiful. So spacious and comfy. I can't wait for you to see it."

"I'm so happy for you, my love. You've worked hard and you deserve this."

"Thanks Gram. So, Mom just called me. Said she's been trying to get a hold of you. Is everything okay?"

"Oh yes, hon. I've just been busy. I'm getting ready to take a trip. I've been shopping, getting supplies I'll need."

"That sounds fun Grams. Where are you going?"

"Well, you know the college kids are getting ready for their spring break, so most of them will be gone. It'll be a dull time with most of them leaving."

Grams starts clicking her dentures. Here we go.

"Some of the girls and a few of the guys are heading for Europe. Lula, Mamie, and I were invited to tag along. We're going to backpack across Europe and stay someplace hostile, although I don't know why they want to stay with angry people. Where's the fun in that?"

"First off, Grams, it's a *hostel*, which is sort of like a hotel, not 'hostile'. Secondly, you are *not* backpacking across Europe."

"Bethie, it's fine. The kids are cool with it. We can see a lot of the sights, party down at all the hotspots, sleep under the stars, when we aren't staying with angry people. We can be free!"

I blew out a breath and counted to ten.

"Grams, no! Don't make me call Mom. You know she can be there before you can even get your hiking boots tied."

"Oh Bethie, you wouldn't!"

"Yes, Grams, I would. If you want to go somewhere, why don't you come see me? I have plenty of room."

"Maybe I could do that. Any good parties with hot guys there?" Of course, that would be Gram's number one priority.

"Not sure, Grams. I haven't had time to check out the town yet. I've been busy unpacking and getting the house in order."

"Okay, honey. I'll think about it and get back to you. Let's not mention this conversation to your mom, alright? Just tell her

I'm fine and I'll call her soon."

"Alright Grams. Let me know when you plan to visit. Love you."

"Love you too, honey."

When I got off the phone, I texted my mother to let her know Grams was fine and would be in touch, then called out to Gracie.

"Gracie, I need to run to town and pick up a few groceries. Would you like to ride along?"

"Sure Beth. Let's go."

I walked into the kitchen and grabbed my purse and shopping list. We left the house and once Gracie was secure in the back seat, we started off.

"Have you heard anything out of Bart since this morning?" I asked Gracie.

"No, Beth, and I'm worried about him. I really hoped we could have found something out for him. He's so sad."

"I know, Gracie. We'll keep looking for something. Not sure what to look for or where to look next. I'd planned to Google Bart and Loralee later. See if there's anything there. Maybe even go to the library and look in the archives to see if the story is in some of the old newspapers. Maybe they will give us a lead to finding Loralee."

"That's a good idea, Beth."

"Thanks, Gracie."

"So, what was Grandma up to now? I heard you on the phone with her."

I started telling Gracie about Gram's latest plan.

"Grandma is a hoot, Beth! I just love her! She lives her life to the fullest."

"Yeah, she definitely lives outside the box. If she doesn't slow down, Mom is going to lock her *in* that box." Gracie and I chuckled.

We pulled up in front of Stein's Market and I shut the car off then turned to look at Gracie.

"So, Gracie, you told me awhile back that this was a magical town. Does that mean we can have conversations in front of other people without me getting put in a straitjacket?"

"Yes, Beth. The people here know I can talk. There's so much about this town you've yet to discover. Just give it time and try not to freak out when you see or hear things that don't quite seem normal to you."

"Like what?"

"You'll see eventually once the people get to know you. Just keep an open mind. You know, like you've done with Bart."

"Okay, Gracie. I'll trust you and try not to freak out."

I just wasn't sure how many more of the unexpected surprises I could take before my mind blew wide open.

We got out of the car and headed into the market. I grabbed a shopping cart and my list.

As we were browsing the aisles, someone called out to me.

"Beth! Gracie! Hello! How are you?"

I turned to find Anna approaching us.

"Anna, hi! I'm fine. How are you?"

"Oh, busy, busy. So, how's the house? Getting settled in?"

"Yes, I am. I love the house. Thank you for arranging to have the internet and utilities on. That was one less thing I had to deal with. I've even met one of my neighbors. Mr. Romano?"

"Oh yes, Guiseppe. He's great! He owns the Italian restaurant here in town. The food, oh! Deliziosa!" Anna kissed her fingers and threw them in the air.

"He invited me to come in and have a meal. He also wants to speak with me about possibly taking over his accounting for the restaurant."

"My husband mentioned that. He told me Guiseppe had called him earlier. Definitely go in to see him soon. His wife has taken over the bookkeeping for the business since their last accountant left but they are always booked solid and I know she'd much rather be in the restaurant working, not taking care of the finances. You'll love Francesca—that's his wife."

"We talked about me coming in next Monday. Guiseppe said the restaurant is closed then and we could talk business without interruptions."

"Beautiful! I've been meaning to call you, but with the kids and the business, I've been so busy. I was wondering, do you have plans for this Saturday?"

"Not that I can think of, why?"

"Well, I'm throwing a small get together at my house Saturday evening and I'd like you to come as my special guest. The townspeople are quite curious about you and what better way to introduce you and give you a chance to meet everyone."

"Wow, Anna. I'm honored. Sure, I'll come. It will be great to start meeting people."

"Perfect. How does 6:00 sound?"

"That works. Do you need me to bring anything?"

"Nope! I've got it all taken care of. Casual dress, nothing fancy. Okay, gotta run! See you Saturday!"

"See you, Anna."

I decided to pick up a nice bottle of wine to take with me Saturday. I felt bad showing up empty handed.

Two aisles over, a man placed a call on his cell.

"It's me. She's going to the Wolfsbane house on Saturday."

Chapter Seven

The week flew by. I'd finished up all the client quarterly returns and had finally gotten the rest of the boxes unpacked. Gracie spent her time hanging out with Bart, who had finally reappeared from wherever ghosts go to hang out. He was actually pretty entertaining once he'd gotten over his initial nervousness. I'd hoped Gracie's and my friendship with him would help him in some small way.

Now that the house was coming together and everything was unpacked, Gracie and I decided to go out and explore the town. I had searched the internet for any stories relating to the history of Raven's Glen and, more specifically, anything on Bart and Loralee. I'd found nothing on either. I decided to check out the library while we were out and about today.

When we got to town, I parked my car and Gracie and I started walking. There were all types of interesting shops along Main Street, in addition to the typical ones.

My first stop was a cute little coffee shop called Ground Zero. When I entered, A little bell above the door tinkled announcing my arrival. It smelled heavenly inside!

There were tables and chairs set up with checkered tablecloths and matching seat cushions. Most of the tables were occupied by individuals working on their laptops, or small groups just sitting together chatting. On the walls around the shop were coffee inspired pictures and signs.

Against one wall was a counter containing various plain and flavored creamers, sugar (just in case you preferred to flavor your own coffee), stir sticks, and napkins. The opposite wall contained bags of ground coffee you could purchase, in addition to bins of coffee beans in every flavor you could imagine. It was sort of like a candy store for coffee addicts. Since I was in no hurry, I browsed the selections while waiting for the line at the counter to die down a little.

The counter to order coffee by the cup was at the back of the shop. Overhead was an extensive menu board, listing coffees, cappuccinos, espressos, and macchiatos, along with additional flavorings to add. I ordered a medium vanilla caramel cappuccino with a chocolate spritz.

The woman behind the counter took my order and handed it to one of the younger girls who were in charge of making the orders. After I'd paid, the woman looked at me and smiled.

"You must be our new resident Anna was talking about. Welcome to my shop. I'm Emma Martinez."

I smiled back at her and said, "Hello, Ms. Martinez. I'm Beth Woodson. It's nice to meet you. I absolutely love your shop and you will definitely be seeing more of me! I had a sampler pack of your coffee in the gift basket Anna Wolfsbane had given me when I moved in. Thank you so much."

"It's no problem, my dear. Glad you enjoyed it and, please, call me Emma."

"And you can call me Beth."

"Anna tells me you're an accountant?"

"Yes. I run an accounting business from home."

"I'm not sure if you've heard, but the accountant we had here moved last year. I'd be interested in talking to you about taking over my payroll and my books. I'm so busy here all the time that most of my free time is spent on making sure the accounting is kept current."

"Thank you! I'd love to speak with you about it."

She handed me my coffee and asked, "What do you think about the town so far?"

I took a sip of my coffee and swore I'd died and gone to Heaven. It was simply divine!

"I haven't had much time to explore, what with moving in and getting unpacked. My dog, Gracie, and I decided to go and check things out today. This is my first stop."

"Well, welcome! If you'll give me your number, I will call you to set up a time to go over my books."

"Sure thing," I said.

She handed me a piece of paper and a pen. I wrote my information down and handed it to her.

"Have a wonderful day, Beth, and do come back to see us."

"I most definitely will. Thank you."

I turned to leave and as I got to the door, an older gentleman was just coming in. He held the door open for me, smiling.

"Thank you," I said.

Gracie, who decided to wait outside for me, stood, hackles raised and emitting a low growl. The man looked over at her as he continued to hold the door.

I'd never known Gracie to exhibit any type of aggression toward anyone, so, I asked her, "What was that about?" as she and I continued walking down the sidewalk to check out the other shops.

"There's just something about that man I don't like, Beth."

"Well, he's gone now. Let's continue."

Instead of going into the coffee shop, the man who had held the door for Beth released it and turned to walk in the opposite direction as Beth.

*****

Gracie and I walked along one side of the street. I was amazed at all the shops the town had. We passed Zelinda's Teapot, a cozy little tearoom, Between the Pages, a bookstore offering new and used books, Blessed Bee Quilts and Supplies, a quilting, fabrics, and craft store, and Ollie's Office Supplies, a store I'd also be a frequent visitor to.

The block ended at the town square where the government buildings were. Here we saw the Municipal Courthouse, the police station, the post office, the local newspaper office, and the library.

There was a traffic roundabout with a statue in the center. The statue depicted a man sitting astride a horse with a dog sitting on the bottom next to them. A plaque below gave the man's name and a brief history. I assumed he was the founding father of this town, but I didn't stop to read the plaque.

Gracie and I headed to the library. It was a three-story brick building sitting atop a carved limestone foundation. Chiseled above the entrance were the words 'Raven's Glen Public Library. Est. 1890'.

We pulled open the double doors of a small foyer where another set of doors led inside. This had to be one of the biggest libraries I'd ever been in. The center was open so that you could look up and see all the way up to the inside of the domed roof. Stained glass panels made up the walls of the dome. There were railings circling each floor. I could see some people reading, sitting in chairs that were set up against the railings.

Several patrons were checking out books at the desk. Others were milling around, browsing the aisles.

I walked up to the desk, waiting in line. When it was my turn, I explained to the librarian that I was new in town, and I'd like to get a card. Then I told her I was doing some research and asked if they had copies of any old newspapers.

She told me they had copies stored on their servers dating back to the library opening and dedication ceremony. She put my information into her computer to sign me up for a card, then walked me over to the patron computers and showed me how to access the information I was looking for and how to search for anything specific. If I needed to print anything off, there was a five cents per page charge. I could pick the pages up at the desk. I thanked her and started searching for any information on Bart and Loralee.

Gracie was lying on the floor next to me while I searched. I finally found several articles relating to Bart and Loralee. One was an engagement announcement. I browsed through the extensive information detailing everything about the soon to be bride and groom's family, wedding and honeymoon plans.

The next article I pulled up talked about the accident in which Loralee and the preacher were killed when the buggy overturned. As I browsed the pictures, I gasped. Among the people shown helping was a very familiar face. Gracie stood up when she heard my rapid intake of breath, on alert for any danger.

"What is it, Beth?" Gracie asked me, her voice laced with concern.

"I've found an article relating to Loralee's accident. Gracie, look at this picture. Does anyone stand out to you?"

Gracie looked up at the picture on display.

"It looks like Guiseppe, doesn't it?"

Gracie chuckled and said, "It does, indeed, Beth."

Confused by why my dog thought this humorous, I asked her for clarification.

"It's nothing, Beth, really."

"I guess it could be some relation to him," I mused. "I mean, he's not *that* old!" I chuckled.

Gracie didn't respond.

There were a few other articles about the funeral arrangements for Loralee, as well as an obituary. A few days later, there was an ad searching for a new preacher, and lastly, fifty years later, an obituary for Bart.

Not really finding any new or helpful information, I logged out, thanked the librarian, then Gracie and I left.

On the way out of the doors, the same man from the coffee shop was outside, once again looking as if he were coming into the library.

"Hello again," he smiled.

"Hello," I answered.

"We seem to keep running into each other."

"Yes, it does seem that way."

Gracie started growling yet again. I reached down to touch her to let her know it was okay.

He offered nothing in the way of an introduction, merely saying, "Well, have a nice day," and went into the library.

"Wow! Twice in one day," I said to Gracie. "Coincidence?"

Gracie responded with a snort.

The man stepped in between the two sets of doors and, as soon as Beth was out of sight, made a call.

"I think that girl and her dog may be a problem. We may have to take care of that."

Chapter Eight

It was Saturday evening, and I was putting the finishing touches on my makeup, in preparation to go to Anna's. Gracie walked into the bathroom.

"Are you ready to meet everyone, Beth?"

"I'll admit, Gracie, I'm a bit nervous, but I'll be fine."

Finished getting ready, I went into the kitchen, grabbed the bottle of wine from the wine fridge and picked up my purse. Bart was standing by the breakfast nook, staring out the window.

"Bart, are you sure you don't want to go with us to Anna's? I feel bad leaving you here by yourself."

I wasn't sure if Anna and her guests would be able to see Bart, but really didn't feel right going off and leaving him behind.

"No Miss Beth. I'll be fine. I just don't think I'd be very good company right now. You and Gracie go along and have fun."

"Are you sure? Maybe you'll feel better getting out of the house for a bit. You're more than welcome to go with us."

"I'm sure Miss Beth. I just need a little time by myself, and I'll be right as rain."

I reluctantly agreed and Gracie and I went out to the car.

I pulled up in front of Anna's house and Gracie and I went to the front door. Before I could ring the bell, the door opened.

"Beth! Come in, please!" Anna said as she hugged me. "Everyone is here and quite excited to meet you!"

I handed Anna the bottle of wine as she steered me inside. Her house was very tastefully decorated. Pictures of the kids at various ages lined the staircase, as did family photos and pictures of what I assumed to be Anna and her husband.

We went into the dining room where everyone had congregated. A variety of different dishes were lined up on the sideboard, along with desserts.

Anna said, "Everyone, this is Beth and her wonderful companion Gracie. Beth, Gracie, this is everyone."

A round of 'hellos' and 'nice to meet you' went around the room. I recognized a few people from town and saw Giuseppe standing off to the side talking with a few other men. He smiled and nodded to me.

"Don't worry," Anna said to me. "I'll take you around and introduce you to individuals in a little bit."

"Where are the kids tonight?" I asked Anna.

"They are staying with my mom. Daisy was pretty upset when she heard you and Gracie were coming, but Micah said he didn't want to hang around at some boring old people party. Kids!"

"Daisy sure does like Gracie, and I know the feeling is mutual," I told her.

Anna took the bottle of wine into the kitchen to open, after inviting everyone to dig in.

When she came back into the dining room, she walked over to me, arm in arm with a tall, dark-haired man. He seemed familiar but I couldn't remember where I'd seen him before. Then it came to me. The picture in the archives about Loralee's accident. He was in the picture too.

Well, one of his ancestors. Probably. No, definitely. Get a grip, Beth!

"Beth, I'd like you to meet my husband Jeremiah or Jerry. Jerry, this is Beth."

Jeremiah shook my hand and said, "I've heard so much about you. It's nice to finally meet you, Beth. Anna speaks very highly of you."

Flattered by Jeremiah's statement, I responded, "Thank you. It's very nice to meet you as well. You have a lovely home and I'm honored to have been invited."

Anna let go of Jeremiah and looped her arm through mine. She took me around the room introducing me to everyone else.

I was halfway through my dessert and talking to a few of the ladies when I heard the front door open and then close. A few seconds later another tall dark-haired man walked into the dining room.

He was wearing a black leather jacket, a faded pair of blue jeans, which he filled out quite nicely, and a black Henley shirt. He took his jacket off and, whoa! Tight jeans, bulging biceps! The only thing ruining the whole package was the scowl on his face. He didn't seem too thrilled to be here. Anna looked up from her conversation with me, Francesca Romano, and Elsa Stein. She excused herself, stood and went over to the newcomer.

"Derek! So glad you made it! Let me introduce you to our newest resident."

She led Derek over to where I was sitting at the table.

"Derek, this is our newest resident Beth Woodson. Beth, this is my brother Derek. He's a sheriff's deputy here in Raven's Glen."

Derek looked at me with the most gorgeous amber colored eyes but didn't offer any other acknowledgement of my presence, aside from a slight nod of his head. As for me, I couldn't help but acknowledge *his* presence. It felt as if the room temperature had increased tenfold. I really needed to get a handle on my hormones before I started panting or drooling over this tightly packed wall of muscles and testosterone.

"Rough night little brother?" Anna asked him.

He kept his eyes trained on me while he answered Anna's question. "You could say that."

"Well come on! Let's get you something to eat, I'm sure you must be starving and there's plenty left."

Derek finally tore his eyes away from me and disappeared into the kitchen with Anna. I turned back to the conversation I was having with Elsa and Giuseppe's wife Francesca.

"So, Beth, are you still meeting with my Giuseppe about taking over our accounting? You come highly recommended by Anna, and I really would like to get back to the customer side. Bah! Stuck in an office all day! Not for me!"

I couldn't figure out why Anna was singing my praises to everyone. We'd only just met a month ago.

"Yes, Francesca, I'm coming in around 11 Monday morning."

"Ahhh! Fabulosa! I know you will be the answer to my prayers!"

Elsa added, "We could probably use some help with the grocery mart's books as well. Frank and I usually do them, but it would free us up for better things to have a professional. I will talk to Frank."

"That is so kind of you, Elsa! Thank you so much!"

Wow! At this rate, I'd double my client list in no time.

Anna and Derek came back into the dining room. I kept sneaking glances at Derek, but he caught me every time. Even though he and Anna were having a conversation, his eyes were like laser pointers that had locked onto me, and I started feeling guilty of something, like I'd committed some sort of crime.

Anna came over and sat back down at the table with Francesca, Elsa, and me. I asked Anna if I could use her restroom.

"Sure! There's a half bath just down that hall past the kitchen doorway. Second door on the right." She pointed in the direction of the hall.

I thanked her, excused myself, and made my way over to the hall. I walked a short distance down and opened the second door, went into the bathroom and locked the door behind me. I didn't need to use the bathroom, just wanted to get away from Anna's brother and his intense stare for a few minutes. I felt like an ant under a magnifying glass in full sunshine. I walked over to the sink and looked in the mirror. My face was flushed a bright red. I turned the sink tap on to cold, washed my hands and patted a little water on my face trying to cool it down.

When I thought I had cooled down sufficiently enough and regained my composure to return to the group, I turned the faucet off, dried my hands, and turned to unlock the door. As soon as I opened it, Derek was standing in the hall, leaning against the wall.

"I'm sorry. I didn't realize you were waiting."

I stepped out to walk past him, but he was blocking the path, and all means of escape. He didn't make any attempt to move out of the way to let me pass, instead stood where he was, leaning against the wall, lazily looking at me.

"If you'll excuse me, I'll just get out of your way," I said, flustered under his stare.

He stood up straight, all 6'3" of him, but I still couldn't get past him in the narrow hall. I looked up at him, wide-eyed, as the hall started closing in on me.

He took a step toward me. I was frozen in place and couldn't move my feet if I wanted to.

"Uh...I...uh...excuse me, please," I squeaked.

Derek was so close I could smell the aftershave he wore and the minty piece of gum he was chewing. Just when I thought I would melt into a sizzling puddle in the floor, he smiled and stepped to his left, freeing up the means of escape. He swept his arm out toward the dining room, not saying a word. I beat a hasty retreat out of the hall and back to safety. My legs were shaking so badly,

I wasn't sure I'd make it.

Anna glanced up at me as I walked back over to the table.

"Beth? Are you okay?" Gracie asked. "Your face is redder than a ripe tomato."

I smiled through quivering lips, my heart keeping a nice calypso rhythm.

Derek came back into the dining room and went over to where the men were.

"Oh yes. I'm fine. Just fine. Everything is fine."

My voice came out like a chipmunk who had just inhaled a balloon full of helium.

The ladies and Gracie looked at me strangely, like I was going to hop up on the table and start stripping off my clothes, while singing show tunes at the top of my lungs. Although as hot as it felt in here right now, I wouldn't mind sinking into a tub full of ice water.

I cleared my throat, sat back down before my legs gave out and reassured them I was fine.

We resumed conversation, but it took me a bit to get my bearings and stop my stomach from turning somersaults. I tried to forget about that strange encounter in the hall with Derek, and just about the time it would start to dissipate, I'd catch Derek glancing over at me. I needed to get out of here and soon!

Anna, unaware of the fact her brother was making me a nervous wreck, topped off her and Elsa's wine glasses and pointed the bottle toward mine. I nodded my head, not sure if I could trust my voice. She was telling us a story about something Micah, her son, had done, but for all I knew she was speaking a foreign language. My brain couldn't focus, knowing Derek was watching me. What's up with him, anyway? Did he get off scaring people or what? I drank the entire glass of wine in one gulp. Again, the ladies looked at me, but said nothing.

It was getting late, so I decided to start making the rounds to say goodnight to everyone. Once I stood up, all the wine hit me. I swayed a little on my feet.

"Beth, are you okay?" Anna asked.

"I think I had a bit more to drink than I realized."

"I'll have Derek drive you home. You can leave your car here and I'll come over to pick you up tomorrow. Francesca, Elsa, and I are going to brunch, and we'd love it if you came too. Seems you're a hit!" Anna smiled.

"Uh, it's okay Anna. I'm not far. Gracie and I can walk."

I wasn't even sure walking was a good idea but given the choice of walking or being in close proximity to Derek, I think walking was a better option. How much had I had to drink? I remembered downing that last glass. Everyone probably thought I was a raging alcoholic.

"Nonsense. Plus, I want to make sure you make it home without any issues. It's a small town, but things still happen here. I wouldn't be able to sleep, knowing you were out there walking alone in the dark." Derek didn't look too thrilled to be appointed my chauffeur.

"I won't be alone. I have Gracie."

Gracie popped her head up and looked at me at the sound of her name.

"Beth, I think Anna is right. Let's have Derek drive us."

"See, even Gracie thinks it's a good idea."

I begrudgingly agreed but hoped I didn't do or say anything stupid or embarrassing in front of this perfect male specimen.

"Hang on a sec. I'll pack you up a container of leftovers to take with you."

She came back out carrying a bag with enough food to feed an army. She handed me the bag and admonished her brother to make sure he got me home safely, which earned her an eye roll from Derek.

"You owe me one for this, Sis," Derek said quietly to Anna, but just loud enough that I heard him. She smacked him on the arm then hugged me and I left with Derek.

We walked out to his car, and he opened the passenger door without a word. He pushed the passenger seat forward to allow Gracie to climb in the back seat, then pushed it back in place for me.

Of course, he drove a car that fit right in with his overload of testosterone--a shiny black '69 'Cuda. Whoa!

He then went around to the driver's side, climbed in, fastened his seat belt and started the car. It roared to life, all eight cylinders, dual exhaust of pure beastly muscle. Sort of like him. I started mentally fanning myself.

He flew down the street and headed toward my house, still not saying anything. I decided to break the ice.

"This is a nice car. I bet it goes fast. Is it hot in here?"

Yeah, I know, lame attempt. He didn't take the bait, remaining silent. Are we there yet? Too bad Grams wasn't here. She'd know how to get him to talk. On second thought...

I tried again. "I'm sorry Anna made you drive us home. I appreciate it though. I know you probably had better things to do than play chauffeur to me. I didn't think I'd had a lot to drink. I would have been fine walking. So how do you like being a deputy? Bet you meet a lot of interesting people."

Oh good lord! Shut! Up! Why was I such a babbling mess? I've never acted like this around anyone. He glanced over at me, probably wishing I'd shut up too. Even Gracie was looking at me like I had just sprouted a second head. It wouldn't surprise me if he stopped the car in the middle of the street and made me get out and walk.

As soon as he pulled in front of my house, he put the car in Park, turned to me and said, "I'm not sure what you're about, but my sister seems to have taken a liking to you. Anna is a very trusting person but I'm not. If you have any plans to cause harm to her or her family, as well as anyone in this town, I'll be all over you."

Boy, those last five words he spoke conjured up some wicked images in my inebriated brain. Focus, Beth.

Then realizing the full gist of what he was saying, I started feeling a bit indignant. Me harm someone? What the crap? Who does he think he is? He doesn't even know me and he's acting like I'm some sort of deranged serial killer!

I opened my mouth to give him a piece of my mind, only I started stuttering, "I-I-I swear, I'm not out to harm anyone. I wouldn't. I really like Anna and she's been a big help to me."

Derek got out and came around to the passenger side. He opened my door to let me out, then pushed my seat forward to let Gracie out too. As we were walking up the steps to my front door, Derek called out.

"I'm watching you, Ms. Woodson." Then he got back into his car and drove off.

Gracie and I went inside. I closed and locked the door, then turned to her and asked, "What was that all about? He acted like I was some sort of criminal."

Gracie said, "He's just being protective of his sister, Beth. He doesn't really know you. I wouldn't give it too much thought."

"I guess, but still…He was just so rude!"

"Just give it time. He'll see what a great person you are."

"I won't lose sleep over it, that's for sure." I did know those amber eyes would be haunting my dreams though.

"What do you say we head to bed? Sounds like we have a busy day tomorrow."

"Sounds good to me, Beth."

I'd noticed Bart wasn't around, but called out goodnight to him anyway, just in case. No response came so I turned off the lights and went to the bedroom to get ready for bed.

*****

She didn't see the man in the woods watching. As soon as the last light popped off in the house, the man made a call.

"She just got home but I couldn't do anything. Capaldi brought her home."

The caller said something, and the man answered, "Don't worry about it. There will be other chances. Just be patient," then he hung up.

Chapter Nine

Sunday morning came too early. Gracie saw me stirring and came over to the side of the bed.

"Good morning, Beth. How are you feeling?"

"Ugh! Like Hell left its calling card and it's inside my head."

I got up to use the restroom and get a couple of aspirins. I knew a cup of coffee would go a long way to taming the native drums banging inside my skull. I really didn't think I'd drunk that much last night. I'd have sworn I only had two glasses of wine.

After a pot of coffee, I was feeling somewhat human again and went in to take a shower. I wasn't sure what time Anna was picking me up but thought it would be somewhat early since it was brunch. I'd just finished drying my hair when I heard a car pull up.

The bell rang and I went to answer. Anna looked especially chipper this morning. She was dressed in a pair of yellow capris and a floral shirt whose flowers matched the yellow of her pants.

"Good morning! I'm not too early, am I?"

"No Anna. I'm ready to go."

Gracie and I got into Anna's SUV. I immediately pulled a pair of sunglasses out of my purse and put them on. The sun seemed overly bright today.

"Sorry about last night Anna. I didn't think I'd drunk that much. It really hit me."

"It's no problem. I should have warned you the wine Cyrus

makes is quite a bit stronger than your average wine. He owns the vineyard here. We'll have to make plans to go out there and take the tour. It's a wonderful time. I'm sure Elsa and Francesca would go with us."

"It definitely packs a punch. I think I was KO'd before round one ended. Where are we having brunch?"

We're meeting the other ladies at the country club restaurant. They have a marvelous brunch every Sunday. I've been so busy lately that I haven't had time to meet up with the girls. You've given me the perfect excuse to take time off. We'll get some food in you, and you'll feel better in no time."

"I hope so. I'd swear I have a metal band from Hell playing a drum solo in my head. Ugh!"

"Speaking of which, how was the ride home? Did my brother make sure you got there safely?"

Not wanting to create problems between Anna and her brother, I said, "Yes, he got me home safe and sound."

"He's single, you know."

Anna looked over at me and smiled slyly before looking back at the road.

"Yeah, I don't think he cares much for me. Not like that, at least. Anyway, I'm not looking for a relationship."

"In my experience, love sneaks up on you when you least expect it."

"And in your brother's case, it would probably sneak up on me, slap me in handcuffs, lock me up and throw away the key."

Little did I know that statement would come back to haunt me in the near future.

Anna chuckled. "Ooooh, I like where this is going!"

She then looked at me and said, "I know he probably seems like a big jerk, and, believe me, he can be. But he's a great guy. He's really protective of me and the kids and comes off kind of harsh but give him a chance. Once he gets to know you, he's fun to be around."

"The town has been having some....uh...issues here lately and he's working night and day trying to figure things out. I keep telling him he's working too hard and needs to cut loose now and then. Unwind, socialize. But until the case is solved, he won't listen. He needs to find a nice girl to settle down with who will force him to relax a bit."

"I don't exactly have the best track record when it comes to men. My ex-husband is the poster child for reasons not to get involved."

"Don't give your ex the power to turn you off men forever, Beth. You deserve someone who will love, respect, and nurture you."

A few minutes later we pulled into a spot in front of the club. People were enjoying the nice day; some were playing tennis and a few golfers were out. My parents would love this.

I told Gracie to be good, we'd be back in a bit, but Anna told me to bring her in.

"We're a very pet friendly community here. They're welcome everywhere."

I opened the back door and let Gracie out. Anna, Gracie, and I walked up the steps into the club entrance. Anna turned to the left, walking through an indoor dining room. She continued walking to a set of doors leading out to the covered patio dining area.

"Everyone is out on the patio. It's such a beautiful day!"

I followed her out toward a table already occupied by the other two ladies. Elsa saw us first and waved us over.

"Anna! Beth! So glad you could join us. Have a seat."

Anna sat next to Elsa on one side of the table, and I sat next to Francesca on the other side. Gracie offered a greeting to Elsa and

Francesca, then laid down near my feet on the patio, basking in the warm morning sun. Elsa called the waiter over to take our order. Half of a pitcher of mimosas sat on the table.

"Help yourself to a mimosa, dear," Francesca told me.

Francesca was dressed in a black silk blouse and tan slacks. Her auburn hair was cut in a sleek bob that fit her perfectly. Elsa was wearing a deep blue summer weight sweater that brought out the blue in her eyes. Her blonde hair was pulled back in a classy, twisted chignon. Sitting with these three perfectly pulled together ladies, I felt like a bag lady in comparison.

"I think I'll stick to water this morning. I seemed to have overdone things last night."

"It's my fault," Anna said. "I forget what a wallop Cyrus's wine packs."

"Oh my, yes," Elsa answered. "A little bit goes a long way."

We all chuckled. Didn't I know that to be true! Not only had I sworn off men, but I've decided to add wine to the list as well.

The waiter came to take our order and after he left, Francesca asked Anna, "Any news from your brother?"

"He hasn't said much, and I didn't have a lot of time to talk to him last night."

"I wish they could find something out about what's going on. We'd all sleep better at night," Elsa responded.

"What is going on? Anna, I know you said your brother is working on a big case. Anything I should be aware of?"

"We don't want to scare you Beth," Francesca said just as the waiter brought us our food.

"But maybe we should tell her. Forewarned and all," said Elsa.

I looked between the three ladies waiting for an explanation.

Anna spoke up. "Francesca's right, Beth. We don't want to scare you, but you do need to be made aware of things that are happening. It seems several townspeople have disappeared. None of them informed their family or friends of unexpected or planned trips. They were just here one day, gone the next without a trace."

"How long has this been going on?"

Elsa said, "What's it been? About seven months or so?"

"About that," Francesca replied.

"Is that why you didn't want me walking home last night?"

"Yes," Anna answered. "We don't know what's going on. The disappearances are so random. No rhyme or reason. I didn't want anything to happen to you. Just make sure when you're home to keep your doors and windows locked and be aware of your surroundings when you're out alone."

"I appreciate it, Anna. I'll keep my eyes open. I always have Gracie with me so she'd know if someone was around who shouldn't be."

Gracie raised her head, looking at me, and added, "I'll be extra vigilant and keep an eye out. Nothing's going to hurt my Beth."

"Thanks, Gracie!"

"That's what friends are for," Gracie answered.

"Let's talk about something happier, shall we?" Elsa asked.

Anna poured herself a mimosa and topped off Elsa and Francesca's glasses.

We talked about different events the town council had planned now that spring was upon us. Several were happening in the next few weeks. The biggest was the spring festival. People came from all over. They had craft booths, entertainment, and lots of food. The ladies went together every year and invited me to accompany them.

"We also have a weekly book club on Tuesday evenings 7 p.m. at the library, Beth. I don't know if you'd be interested, but you should come and join us. It's a good time. We have wine and snacks, and we don't always stay on track. That's when the fun begins," Elsa said, winking at me.

"Sounds like a good time. I'm an avid reader so I'd love to join. I just don't know if I'll be partaking in the wine part though." The ladies laughed.

"Great! Hopefully we'll see you Tuesday then."

Francesca lowered her voice and said, "Well, well. Look what the goat dragged in."

We all looked toward the doors going inside. There was a man coming out to the patio area dressed in a three-piece suit.

"Who is he?" I asked.

"That is our honorable mayor. And I use the word 'honorable' lightly," Elsa answered. "The troll!"

"Not to speak ill of others, but he's just so…."

"Ick?" Francesca finished for Anna.

"That works," Anna replied.

"How that man ever got elected once, much less re-elected two times is beyond me."

"I agree," said Francesca. "He went from living under a bridge to getting elected as mayor and wearing designer suits and driving an expensive sports car."

Had he been homeless? Sounded like it if he'd been living under a bridge. I'm not sure I understand the aversion to him. Sounded like a rags to riches story to me.

"What's wrong with him?" I asked. "He sounds like he's done very well for himself if he was homeless and living under a bridge."

The ladies looked at me strangely for a second before Francesca continued.

"He comes off as so charming and only looking out for the best interests of his constituents, but there's something about him that I can't place my finger on. He's like a snake oil salesman, that one. He's very condescending and smug but tries so hard to disguise it with charm."

"He sounds like my ex-husband. I wonder if they're related."

"He's just so smarmy. I feel like I need to bathe in bleach water after being anywhere in his vicinity. And, oh great, here the troll comes now," said Elsa.

The mayor walked over to our table.

"Ladies, looking lovely as usual. Beautiful day, beautiful women. What more could one ask for?" he said with a toothy smile that reminded me of a shark, then he looked at me.

"And who is this lovely young lady? I don't believe I've had the pleasure of making your acquaintance."

"This is Beth Woodson, Mayor. She just moved to town. Beth, this is our mayor Johann Wilson," Anna answered.

"Well, it's always nice to have a fresh pretty face here. How are you enjoying our little town? Finding your way around okay?"

He grabbed up my hand and held it a bit too long for my liking. He then kissed the top of it. Uh, ewww! It was like having a toad lick my skin. Gracie looked at him and bared her teeth. He didn't seem to notice. I get it now. I quickly pulled my hand away.

"Any updates on the missing townsfolk Mayor?" Elsa asked.

"We're working diligently to figure out what's going on, Mrs. Stein. In due time I'm sure the mystery will come to light, and we'll find our much-loved missings. Don't you worry your pretty head about it though. I have every confidence that our fine officers are investigating things thoroughly. We'll have answers soon."

He brought his wrist up and looked at the time on what seemed to be a very expensive wristwatch. "Ladies, it's been a pleasure, but I must run now. If you ever need anything, anything at all,

Ms. Woodson, my door is always open. Have a fantastic day!" And with that, he was gone.

"Okay, he is just a bit creepy," I said to the other ladies. "And he kissed my hand. Uh ewww! I see what you mean. I feel like I need to go wash my hand in boiling water now."

The ladies chuckled.

"He sure high tailed it out of here when you brought up the disappearances," said Francesca.

"Yep, old Johann Wilson. Thinks he's a master charmer and ladies' man, but any talk of serious business, especially from women, and he takes off like the devil's chomping his coattails," said Elsa.

"He couldn't get a date with a desperate goat, but he sure thinks he's every woman's dreamboat and we swoon in his presence," Francesca snarked, throwing the back of her hand against her forehead.

"To quote our friend Beth, 'Uh, eww!" Elsa said and we all laughed.

We were finishing up brunch when Derek walked up to our table. "Ladies," he said to all of us.

I looked up at him and could feel all the blood rushing to my face. He was in full uniform, and boy did he fill it out in all the right places. I gulped. The temperature must have suddenly shot up out here, since I could feel the sweat starting to form on my forehead. What is it with me when this man is in the vicinity that makes me lose any and all control over my senses?

He looked back at me, his cool expression giving nothing away. I squirmed in my seat a little until he finally looked at his sister.

"This is a surprise! What's on your mind, little brother?" Anna asked, grinning like a Cheshire cat.

Derek looked back at me, held out a jacket and said, "I think you left this in my car last night, Ms. Woodson."

"Oh. I...I'm so sorry. Yes. Thank you, deputy. I didn't realize. I'm so sorry."

See? I can't even manage a complete or coherent sentence.

For the life of me, I couldn't raise my arm to accept the jacket from his hand. I could only sit there and stare at him. He held the jacket out a little farther toward me and Francesca reached up, taking it on my behalf. She draped it over the arm of my chair.

"That was very nice of you, Derek, to bring it all the way out here. You could have just given it to me later this evening," Anna smirked.

"I was in the neighborhood," Derek answered. He touched the brim of his hat to us and said, "Have a nice day, ladies," then turned and sauntered off.

Once he was gone, Anna burst out laughing.

"In the neighborhood, my left foot!" Anna laughed. "He knew we were going to be here."

The other ladies giggled as Anna continued. "Me thinks my brother doth show interest in the fair maiden Beth!"

"I...well...uh...no. He...uh...he was just being nice!"

Elsa dived in. "And me thinks the lady doth protest too much!" The three of them dissolved into a fit of laughter.

Soon it was time to leave. Anna had to take me to get my car, as she was meeting with a client, and Elsa and Francesca, who rode together in Elsa's car, were going to an afternoon matinee. Stein's Market was closed on Sundays and Francesca didn't work at Giuseppe's on Sundays. We paid our bill and said our goodbyes, with Elsa reminding me of their book club meeting on Tuesday.

Anna, Gracie and I headed out to Anna's SUV. As we started outside, an older man held the door for us.

"Have a fabulous day, ladies," he said.

Gracie let out a low growl.

Anna and I thanked him and continued to her car.

"I wonder who that was. I've never seen him here before, but he seems familiar," Anna told me.

"I keep running into him, no matter where I go," I answered. "Gracie does not like him. Every time we see him, she growls, as you saw."

Anna chewed her bottom lip for a second with a concerned look on her face, then shook her head and said, "Oh well, I'm sure he's okay. He seemed to have been right at home at the club. Maybe he's a visiting relative or something. I know I've seen him somewhere before though. I'll have to think about it."

Anna started the car, backed out and headed for the exit.

The man stood inside the entrance doors of the club and watched them leave.

Chapter Ten

Once I picked up my car and got home, I decided a nice long nap was in order. While the food and aspirin worked wonders on my headache, I was sapped.

"Gracie, I'm going to lay down for a bit. Do you need to go out before I do?"

"I'd like to go outside and explore, if you don't mind. Bart's feeling better and said he'd go with me."

"Are you sure you'll be okay outside if I'm asleep? You won't get lost, will you?"

"No. Bart knows his way around pretty good. I'll be fine. If we come back before you're up, we can hang out on the porch." I reluctantly agreed to let Gracie out.

"Don't go far and be careful. Are you sure you don't want me to leave the door open for you?"

At some point in the future, I should think about having a doggy door installed. That way Gracie could go out whenever she wanted to.

"We'll be fine, Beth. Besides, didn't Anna tell you to lock your doors when you were home? Go enjoy your nap."

I opened the back door and let Gracie out then put a bowl of fresh water on the porch for her. I went to the living room and lay down on the couch.

An hour later, I was awakened by Bart. He was surrounded by a red glow. I sat up on the couch and asked, "What's wrong, Bart? What's happened?"

"Oh Miss Beth. It was dreadful, just dreadful I tell you. Gracie and I were down by the creek and a man came walking up. I've never seen him in these parts before. He started talking to me and Gracie. Gracie must have sensed something about him was off, so she started growling."

"Next thing I knew, he threw some kind of collar around Gracie's neck. It was attached to a long pole. She was fighting it and trying to get loose. Then the man did something to her with a gadget he pulled out of his pocket, and she dropped to the ground, out like a stone. He put her in a cage on top of a wagon and took her. I didn't know what to do so I came to get you."

I sprang up off the couch, now wide awake and panicked.

"What did he look like? Which way did they go? Oh, Bart, what am I going to do?"

I started crying, which caused Bart to become even more upset. Piles of M&Ms were stacking up behind him.

"I am so sorry Miss Beth. I tried to stop him, but it was no use. He went right through me like I wasn't even there, but he saw me. He told me I'd do best to forget what I saw if I knew what was good for me. But what can he do to me?"

"What did he look like?"

"He was older. Thin. Not too tall. Had gray hair that looked like it hadn't seen a comb in years. He had on jeans and a sweater and was wearing some kind of big, long coat."

The description sort of matched Guiseppe, but his hair usually wasn't unkempt. Then I thought back to the man Anna and I had seen earlier as we were leaving the clubhouse, the same man who kept popping up everywhere I went. Gracie didn't like him, and she'd said as much. Could it be him? They sounded very similar.

"Which way did he go, Bart?"

"He set off down the path in the woods. How he moved so fast with that wagon is beyond me. I was going to follow them, but the man threw something toward me then it's like I was frozen in place. I couldn't even blink my eyes. After the man had been gone about thirty minutes, whatever it was wore off, so I rushed back here to get you."

"I need to call Anna. Maybe she'll know what to do."

I ran to the kitchen and dug my phone out of my purse. It took my shaky hands a few tries, but I finally got Anna's number pulled up. She answered on the second ring.

"Hi Beth!"

"Oh Anna! Someone has taken Gracie. Some man came out of the woods behind my house and grabbed her."

"Sit tight Beth. I'll be there in five minutes. I'm going to call Derek."

"Anna, A sheriff's deputy is not going to concern himself with a missing dog."

"Trust me. He will take this very seriously. I'll explain when I get there."

I paced around the house until I heard Anna's car pull up. I opened the front door and once Anna was on the porch, she pulled me into a hug.

"Beth, I am so sorry. I called Derek. He's on his way over to get some information from you, then he is going to search the woods. We'll find Gracie. Did you see the man who took her? Did he hurt you?"

"I'm fine, but why would he take Gracie? What does he want with her? She's never bothered anyone."

We went inside and Anna sat me on the couch. She went into the kitchen, made a pot of coffee, and soon returned with two mugs. She sat on the couch next to me to wait for Derek.

Soon there was a knock on the door and Anna got up to answer.

She walked in with Derek, who was still in full deputy uniform. He sat in the chair across from the couch as Anna sat back down next to me.

"Ms. Woodson, when did you realize your dog was gone?" Derek asked.

"I was awakened from a nap by..uh..." I looked at Anna.

"Beth," said Anna, "it's okay. Tell him the whole story without fear of thinking you sound crazy. Trust me."

I blew out a breath, wiped my eyes on a tissue Anna handed me and began.

"This is going to sound crazy. There's a…uh…man that lives here in the house. He told me."

"A man? And what would this man's name be? Would he be available to answer a few questions?" Derek asked.

"Beth, I didn't know you had someone living here with you. You haven't mentioned anything about it," Anna said.

"Well, actually, he's the one who built this house. Gracie and I have been helping him try to find his fiancé. He and Gracie went outside to explore while I napped. He was the one who woke me up about an hour later to tell me someone took Gracie."

With that last part, I started crying again.

Anna took my hand and asked, "Do you mean Bart?"

I whipped my head up to look at Anna.

"You know Bart?"

"Of course, sweetie. We all know him. We haven't seen him in a while though. We thought he'd moved on after his fiancé….well, that's a story for another time."

Derek nodded in agreement. "Please continue."

I was now dumbfounded. Anna and Derek both knew about Bart? I pinched myself on the arm. Yep, that hurt like a mother. Anna looked at me.

"It's okay, Beth. Finish your statement then we'll have a nice long talk."

I told him what Bart had told me about the man throwing something, then Bart feeling like he'd been frozen into place and had been unable to follow the man and Gracie. I also described the man as Bart had described him to me.

Derek asked a bunch of questions that I answered fully, since they knew about Bart. When he was finished, he stood and walked toward the kitchen.

"Ms. Woodson, I'm going to head out and start searching for Gracie. Is there anything else I need to know before I go?"

I can't think of anything more than what I've told you. Please find Gracie," I begged him between sobs.

His face softened and he said, "I'll do my best Beth. Stay here with Anna. I'll come back when I'm done." He turned the back doorknob and went out to search.

"Anna, why would someone take her? What if she's hurt or...."

"Shhhhh honey. Don't think about things like that. Think positively. You have to stay strong. Derek is the best and I'm not just saying that because he's my brother."

Anna's phone rang and she looked at the display.

"Hang on a second. It's Elsa."

She walked into the kitchen, spoke on the phone for a few minutes, then returned to the living room.

"Elsa and Francesca are on their way."

"Why? I thought they had plans."

"They decided to postpone it. I called them on the way here and told them what had happened. You need us more. We take care of our own here. You're one of us now. When you hurt, we all hurt."

I couldn't do anything else but sob.

Twenty minutes later, Elsa and Francesca arrived. Anna let them in, and they both gathered me in a hug.

"Oh, you poor thing. You must be worried sick," said Elsa.

"We rushed right over as soon as we heard. We couldn't let you go through this alone. You have us three. You lean on us as much as you need to," added Francesca.

"What happened? How did Gracie get picked up?" asked Elsa.

Anna asked me if she could tell the story and I nodded my agreement. When she finished, I wiped my face with yet another tissue and asked, "Will you please tell me how everyone knows about Bart? You all act like I'm talking about a real person, sorry Bart, a *living* person instead of a ghost. And, Anna, why is your brother treating my dog's disappearance like a missing person?" Anna, Elsa, and Francesca looked at each other. Anna drew a deep breath then proceeded to answer me.

"How much has Gracie told you about this town Beth?"

"Not a lot. She said the woman I adopted her from was a witch. Although she was a puppy, she was actually quite old and stayed in puppy form until I took her. She told me this is a magical town and to keep an open mind. I know this sounds like something straight out of a fantasy novel, but it's true."

Francesca said, "Okay, keeping those words in mind, we'll tell you a little about the town. Just brace yourself and be prepared. Gracie was correct when she told you this is a magical town. Each of us are magical beings, but some of us are, how should I put this, misfits?" Anna and Elsa nodded.

"What do you mean?"

Elsa continued. "Here goes—-my husband Frank and me? We're actually laboratory creations. A doctor built us out of body parts from the…er…deceased."

"What?!? You mean like Shelley's *Frankenstein*?"

"Yes, dear, exactly like that. Frank was the doctor's first semi-success story. Have you ever noticed the Velcro strips he wears? That's what holds him together. My creation was a much-improved process. I'm actually stitched together."

I felt dizzy and sick, and I don't think it was because of my hangover.

"Francesca and Giuseppe? They're vampires. Neither he nor Francesca drink blood or sleep in coffins. They don't turn into bats, don't have aversions to crucifixes, sunlight, or holy water. That's all Hollywood hype. Sure, a stake to the heart would kill them—as it would anyone. As a matter of fact, Giuseppe can't stand the sight of blood. He faints!"

"And can you imagine Italian food without garlic? Ha!" Francesca added.

"Ok, Anna. What are you?"

"Ahem," Anna cleared her throat. "Jerry and I are lycanthropes. Uh, werewolves."

"Werewolves? Okay, yeah. Sure. Is this some kind of distraction game? Keep my mind off Gracie by telling me wild stories?"

"Unfortunately, no. It's the truth Beth," Anna replied. "We are misfits, if you will, because my whole family are vegetarians. The dog park, as you called it, where I first met you? That was actually a children's park and playground, which is why I was there that day. I was letting the kids burn off some energy before my son's game. Some, but not all, of the dogs you saw were, in fact, were-children in their natural forms."

"And, for the record, we don't tear off our clothes and run wild during a full moon. Lord knows the kids grow out of their clothes fast enough. Jerry and I can barely keep up now. Can you imagine if we all had to buy new clothes after a full moon cycle?"

"To answer your original question about how we know Bart? We were all friends. We were on our way to the wedding when we came upon an overturned buggy. Jeremiah and Giuseppe were two of the men helping at the scene. They were both a lot younger then. We all were. Frank and Elsa didn't live here yet. Poor Bart was there when they found Loralee, Bart's fiancé. She'd been crushed beneath the buggy. He was so devastated," said Francesca.

"I see. That explains why everyone looked at me when I whistled for Gracie in the park. And the pictures I found in the library archives about Loralee's accident where they showed two men who looked like Jerry and Guiseppe. I just thought they were some ancestors of them both. So, I have a scared ghost, vegetarian werewolves, non-blood drinking vampires, a Velcroed Frankenstein and his bride, and a talking dog as friends?"

I looked at the three of them, smiled widely, then passed out.

When I came to, Anna was holding a wet washcloth on my forehead.

"There you are love. Come on. Open your eyes."

I looked at Anna and saw the worried crease between her brows.

"I must have fainted. I've never fainted before in my life."

"It's understandable, sweetie. You've had a terrible shock, then an overload of crazy information," said Francesca.

Wasn't that the understatement of the year!

"I feel just terrible. We shouldn't have divulged so much information in such a short time span. Please forgive us," Elsa said nervously.

"I'm fine, ladies, truly. And yes, that was a lot of information to take in all at once. I guess that's why Gracie told me to keep an open mind."

"You aren't afraid of us, are you?" Anna asked.

"Not at all. None of you have ever caused me any harm or led me to believe you would."

"Oh lord no. We like you. You're one of us. We'd never cause you any harm," Elsa said.

"Ok. Anything or anyone else I should know about?"

"Well, one of the missings is Seamus McGregor. He owns the bar here in town. He's a leprechaun. He's allergic to gold though. Imagine, a leprechaun without a pot of gold," Francesca told me.

There's the leprechaun! Wonder if he rides around on a unicorn?

"And as you know," Francesca continued, "our mayor is a troll. He used to live under the bridge at the lake. Then there's Cyrus, the one who owns the winery. He's a mummy but has a wee bit of a problem keeping his wrappings on."

"We have Sarah the siren who lives in the lake community in Raven's Glen. She has laryngitis so she is unable to sing. And she does not lure the lake boaters to their demise. That's an old wives tale anyway. She's usually the headliner of our spring festival, but with her laryngitis, she can't sing. Her doctors say it's vocal polyps or something like that. The festival entertainment hasn't been the same without her. Let me think, what else…Oh, Emma who runs the coffee shop? She's an angel."

"Uhhhh…." My vision started going fuzzy around the edges.

Elsa cut Francesca off, saying, "But we'll save some of the 'everyone else' part for another time. We don't want to further overwhelm her, do we Francesca?" She patted Francesca's hand, while giving her a warning look.

"Oh, of course. Sorry! Sometimes I get carried away!"

"Then tell me this, is everyone in this town a misfit?"

"We're all magical beings, Beth. We don't like the term 'monsters'. But not everyone is a misfit. "

"So, Anna. If you're a werewolf, does that mean Derek is too?"

Anna's face reddened. "Yes, he is. But he isn't a meat eater either. And being a lycanthrope is why he makes a great deputy. His sense of smell is ten times more powerful than the greatest tracking dog in the world. And I'm not comparing my brother to a dog. Just his sense of smell."

"Since Derek has been unable to track down this monster, yes, monster, who's taking off with the residents of this town, he thinks he may be dealing with someone who's familiar with our situations and knows how to sneak around or among us without detection. If it were a normal situation, Derek would have caught him mere seconds after our first resident went missing. This is why the case bothers Derek so much. None of us know who or what we're dealing with."

I thought about this for a while and looked at the expectant, yet worried faces of my friends. "If I find out who took Gracie, they'd better hope invisibility is one of their abilities."

Chapter Eleven

Elsa, Francesca, and Anna decided to stay with me overnight. Jerry had taken his and Anna's kids to her mother's house tonight and Giuseppe kindly brought over food for us from the restaurant. He told me, in light of what had happened, we would reschedule our meeting. Anna stayed in contact with her brother for updates, but he'd found nothing as of yet.

The next morning, we were in the kitchen having a cup of coffee. Anna told us Derek had found and followed Gracie's scent deep into the woods, but it disappeared. He was on his way back to my house, promising to go out again later. Before long, Derek was walking in the back door. He'd been out searching non-stop since yesterday afternoon and I could tell he was exhausted. I took one look at his face and started crying again.

"I'm so sorry Beth. I picked up the scent and followed it for quite a while. Then it's like it just vanished. I won't give up, I swear. I'll do everything I can to bring Gracie back home to you."

The doorbell rang, startling all of us. I wasn't expecting company and really wasn't up for any. Elsa got up and went to answer. A loud voice rang out from the living room, and I knew exactly who it was. As I started to stand and go into the living room, in walks the source of the shouting.

"Jason, what are you doing here? How did you find out where I live?"

"Your friend Paula told me. You won't answer my calls, so I thought I'd just come in person."

I'd have to remember to cross Paula off my Christmas list. I can't believe she would give him any information about me, especially knowing what happened between he and I. She and I had been best friends since high school, long before I met Jason. The betrayal stung.

"You need to leave. You aren't welcome here."

"Nope. Not when I came all this way to find you. See where our new digs are."

Jason looked around and whistled. Anna and Derek looked at him. "Nice! You did us good, baby."

"This is MY house. There is no 'us'. Leave now!"

"And I said no. I have every right to be here."

Derek stepped closer to Jason. His amber eyes were on fire, and you could almost see his muscles quivering in anticipation of a confrontation.

"You heard the lady. Leave!" Derek practically growled.

"I don't know who you are, dude, but I'm her husband."

You could have heard a pin drop in my kitchen. Derek swiveled his head around to me so quickly, his neck popped. Not that he noticed.

"Your *husband,* Miss, or should I say *Mrs.* Woodson?"

"Derek," Anna started. "This man is not…"

"Save it, Sis."

Derek then turned and without another word, left through the back door. Francesca, Elsa and Anna stood there silently gaping at me. I unleashed all my frustration out on Jason.

"Great! Just great! Jason, WE ARE DIVORCED! Period! End of discussion. I am NOT your wife, and you have NO RIGHT to be in my house. So get that through your thick head. It's over! I don't have the time or energy to deal with you right now so GET! OUT!"

He started backpedaling toward the front door, me hot on his heels, or toes in this case. He got to the door, turned and opened it but stopped and turned back to me.

"This ain't over. You need to get your head on straight and… you know what? Forget it. Paula is more of a woman than you'll ever be. But you and your friends are going to be sorry! You want to throw me over for some muscle-bound pretty boy? You just wait and see what happens!"

He turned around, went out and slammed the door behind him. Then I heard a car door slam and car tires squealing out of my driveway.

I felt all the fight leave me and turned to go back to the kitchen. Everyone was still standing there dumbstruck.

"Well, that was unexpected," Elsa spoke up. "I tried to stop him, but he just pushed his way past me and barged right in."

"It's okay, Elsa and I'm sorry," I began. "Jason is my ex-husband, but apparently, he seems to forget about the paper that says just that. His girlfriend dumped him, so he wants to come crawling back to me. Maybe she's smarter than I gave her credit for being. He'll never change, and I can't believe I was too blinded by what I thought was love that I married him. And now my supposed friend is doling out information on me to him. Ugh!"

"It's okay sweetie. Don't let that donkey's behind add to your worries."

"I try not to, Elsa, but he just won't leave me alone!"

We sat around the kitchen talking for the next few hours. Anna made some cheese and mushroom omelets for us, but I wasn't really hungry. I enjoyed having the girls here but right now I really wanted to be alone.

"I just received a text from Derek. He said he went home to shower and rest, then he's going to work. And, sorry Beth, I don't know if I should read this next part."

"Go ahead, you can tell me, Anna. It's probably not nearly as bad as I'm imagining, considering the look on his face when he left. Tell me."

"Well, he says he has real cases to solve and doesn't have time for wild goose chases. That man, I'm going to kill him! He can be so pig headed sometimes!"

"So I guess that means he's not going to look for Gracie anymore?"

"Beth, I don't know. I don't understand what's gotten into him. Don't you worry. Gracie will be back home if we have to find her ourselves." Anna hugged me, which kicked up the waterworks again.

The three of them soon started gathering their things to leave. Anna had to go pick up her kids and Francesca and Elsa were going to their postponed matinee today.

"Thank you all for coming over and taking time away from your families," I told them. "I know you have the kids, Anna. I'm so sorry to have pulled you away from them."

"It's no problem, Beth. Mama always takes the kids every Sunday. She took them last night because Jerry had to work today. The kids just love her and love spending time with her."

"And neither of us have kids," added Elsa, "although Francesca and I are godmothers to Anna and Jerry's kids."

"You call us if anything happens," Francesca said.

"I'll keep you posted if I hear anything from Derek," added Anna. "And I *will* be hearing something from him one way or another. Trust me."

"Try not to worry Beth. Gracie will be home soon," said Elsa.

They all hugged me then left.

I sat down at the kitchen island, put my head down and sobbed for all I was worth.

I heard a voice coming from the corner of the kitchen.

"Miss Beth? Is it okay if I appear?"

I raised my head and answered, "Sure Bart."

Bart partially materialized across the kitchen, hat in hand, turning it around and around by the brim. He was surrounded by an amber glow.

"I wasn't sure how welcome I'd be after losing Gracie."

M&Ms started appearing behind him.

"Bart, it was not your fault. You didn't know someone was going to take Gracie. And you couldn't have stopped them anyway."

"I just feel like it's my fault. We shoulda never went out there. We shoulda waited until you were with us. I can't tell you how terrible I feel. Gracie is my friend and I shoulda been watching out for her."

"Really Bart. It's okay. But I'll tell you this. I'm not going to sit around doing nothing while my dog is in the hands of God knows who. I'm going to go out to the woods myself and start looking for her."

"Miss Beth, I don't think that's a good idea. We don't know who this person is or what they might do if they catch you. I think you should let Anna's brother handle it."

"I don't think Anna's brother is going to bother with it anymore. So, it's up to me to get my dog back. Can you at least show me where Gracie was when that man took her?"

"Miss Beth...."

"Please Bart. You don't have to do anything else. Just get me started by pointing me in the right direction."

"Well, I guess I can show you, but I can't let you go searching by yourself. I may not be much help, but I can get help if something goes wrong."

"Thank you, Bart."

I put my shoes on, grabbed my keys, threw a few water bottles in my backpack, and Bart and I left.

We arrived at the wet weather creek and Bart showed me where he and Gracie were before the man approached them.

"I was standing right about here, and Gracie was over by the creek bank behind you. That man came from the woods directly behind Gracie."

I walked over to where Bart told me the man appeared from.

"Bart! Look! There's a footprint here on the side of the creek bank."

Bart came to inspect it and said, "Well I'll be. You're right Miss Beth! That's right where he came out."

I started searching the area where I found the footprint. I left the creek bed, climbed up the bank and started into the woods. Bart showed me where he was when the man threw something at him that caused him to freeze. I looked around on the ground and found a tiny metal canister, now empty of its contents. I put the canister in my backpack and continued walking. I hoped if I got too far off the path, Bart could lead me back to my house and I wouldn't get lost.

I walked deep into the woods. I thought it strange that the farther I went into the woods, the quieter it became. Everything around me was completely silent. No birds calling back and forth, no small animals scurrying in the underbrush. The air felt heavy, and it didn't help that the woods were so thick they almost blotted out the sun.

"I've got a real uneasy feeling, Miss Beth," Bart said as he floated next to me. "Something doesn't seem right. Maybe we should turn around and go back."

"I'm almost thinking the same thing, Bart."

I just started to turn around and let Bart lead us back out when I saw something out the corner of my eye. Without saying anything to Bart, I walked closer toward what I'd seen.

Hidden amongst the trees was what looked to be an abandoned cabin. Vines and other vegetation had grown up around it, almost completely covering the building. I pulled some of it away from one of the windows, making a mental note to put a pair of gloves in my backpack.

I cupped my hands around my face and peered inside. It was a tworoom building. A small table and two cane back chairs sat next to what I thought was a kitchen sink. A single plate and a cup sat on the table, a fork and knife next to the plate. There was a twin bed in the front corner covered with an old quilt. It looked to have been empty for a while, but something was niggling in the back of my brain.

I sighed and turned around. Bart had floated up next to me at some point.

"It looks abandoned. Like no one has been here in a long time."

"I didn't even know this was here Miss Beth. Wonder whose place this is?"

"I don't know but I guess it's another dead end. Let's head back home."

We got back to my house about an hour later. I was worn out from crying and traipsing through the woods all afternoon.

"I'm real sorry we didn't find anything, Miss Beth."

"It's okay Bart. There's always tomorrow. Right now, I think I'm going to take a shower and go to bed."

"Yes ma'am, Miss Beth. If you need anything, just holler for me. I'll leave you to your shower. Good evening."

"Goodnight, Bart and thanks for your help today." Bart's glow turned pink.

"I didn't do much, but you're welcome." And with that, he popped out.

I was just finishing my shower when the thought that had been teasing the back of my brain came to light. I hurried out, dried off and got dressed, then called out to Bart.

"Hey Bart! Are you around?"

Bart materialized a few seconds later.

"Yes ma'am, I'm here."

"Did you by chance get a good look inside the cabin we found today?"

"I just took a quick peek. Why?"

"Did you notice anything out of the ordinary?"

Bart scratched his head and thought about it for a moment, then shook his head.

"No Ma'am. Not that I remember. Why? What did you see?"

"The plate, utensils, and cup on the table were clean, as was the quilt on the bed. Doesn't that strike you as off? If that cabin was abandoned, why were those items there, clean and ready to use?"

"Now that you mention it, Miss Beth, that stuff was clean. It wasn't dusty or grimy from sitting there for a long time unused. I think you may be onto something."

"I'm thinking we should start watching the cabin until we know who's using it. Who knows? Maybe we'll find the person who took Gracie."

"That could be dangerous, Miss Beth. You don't think we need to tell Miss Anna or her brother?"

"No, it would only worry Anna and her brother wouldn't do anything about it anyway."

"Well, I guess I can accompany you then. But if it's the guy, we need to make a deal that you'll tell Derek."

"Agreed. We'll pick up where we left off tomorrow?"

"Sure thing Miss Beth. Goodnight."

"Goodnight, Bart."

I went to bed, and I was out within seconds.

Chapter Twelve

Even though Derek said he wasn't going to keep looking for Beth's dog, he was out in the woods searching. He knew down to his bones that Gracie's disappearance was tied to the missing townspeople.

He was so mad when he left. He'd assumed Beth was single until her *husband* showed up at her house. What did she see in that guy anyway? Derek had his number as soon as that idiot swaggered into the kitchen. Maybe Beth wasn't as nice as she seemed. Why else would she be tied up with someone like that? His instincts were at war with the scene back in her kitchen. Maybe he shouldn't have stormed out.

He remembered the last time he'd been fooled by a woman, and it didn't end well. He'd met Shaylene at the academy. She was petite with red hair, green eyes, and the fairest complexion he'd ever seen. He fell hard for her the first time he'd laid eyes on her. Her tiny stature belied her strength. She was able to take the six-foot-tall trainer down in the blink of an eye. She also scored high on marksmanship.

After a month together at the academy, Derek asked her out to lunch, which she readily accepted. She wasn't shy and didn't beat around the bush when it came to what she wanted. They ended up back at his place that evening and he was hooked.

Derek was considering proposing to her right after their graduation from the academy. He had the ring and was just biding his time. Over beers one night, he told his friend, also in the academy, of his plans. That was the night his world crashed and burned. Not only was Shaylene already married, but she was quite well known to quite a few officers. Happy birthday to me.

Derek couldn't believe how stupid he'd been to be taken in by a woman like her. He stopped talking to her the next day, ignored her texts and calls. After graduation, she took a position two counties over, but not before hooking up with the academy instructor. It had been seven years since he last saw her.

He hadn't met anyone in a long time that intrigued him the way Beth did. He enjoyed rattling her cage and watching her get flustered.

Derek stopped for a few minutes to scent the air. He kept picking up trace scents of Gracie, but then it was like a wind came along and scattered the smell like dandelion seeds. It was so frustrating, Derek wished he could punch something. Or someone. Where's Beth's husband when you need a good punching bag?

Derek caught another scent of overpowering cologne, then heard the sound of footsteps. He started walking toward the sound and saw Mayor Wilson.

"Hey, Mayor! What are you doing way out here?"

The mayor looked up, startled to see Derek standing there.

"Oh, just out taking a nature walk. Helps to clear my head before work. I could ask the same of you, deputy. Why are you out here traipsing around?"

Derek could tell by the way the mayor was dressed, he wasn't just out for a walk in the woods. One doesn't wear dress shoes to hike. He was acting kind of strange too. Derek decided he'd have to keep an eye on him.

"I had a call about something in the woods," Derek lied. "I told the caller it was probably a deer or a bear. Nothing to worry about. They insisted I come out to check, saying something about tax dollars and all. You know how hysterical these females can get sometimes."

"Boy, do I ever! So did you find anything?"

"No sir. Just the usual woodland animals—squirrels, chipmunks, birds."

"Good! Good! Hey listen. Walk with me a bit. I'm due in the office soon so I thought we'd walk out together."

"I guess I'm done here sir."

"That's my boy!"

Johann slapped Derek on the back. Derek had to suppress a growl.

"Have you had a chance to meet our newest resident? Man, she's one hot little number."

Derek was trying to refrain from jumping on Johann and pounding him into the ground as he said, "Yes. She was at Anna's get together Saturday. I met her husband this morning."

Who does Johann think he is, talking about Beth like that?

"Wow! Never would have pegged her as a married gal. I met her at the country club on Sunday. She was practically all over me. Good thing it was a public place. Lord knows what she would have done in a more private setting, if you know what I mean."

Johann waggled his eyebrows up and down. The Beth he was describing didn't sound like the Beth Derek had met a couple of times. Who knows, though? People could fool you. He just didn't get that sense from Beth and his instinct was usually spot on, even if she did have questionable taste in men. Johann was unaware of the anger rising up in Derek. If he said one more word about Beth, Derek didn't think he'd be able to control himself any longer. Thankfully, the mayor changed the subject.

As they walked, the mayor started asking about the missing people case and if Derek was making any headway on it.

"Any leads yet?" he asked.

Derek didn't like or trust Johann and even if he was standing here in front of Johann with a suspect in handcuffs, he wouldn't divulge any information to him.

"I'm investigating any and every possible outlet, Sir."

They had reached the small pull-off area where Derek had parked his cruiser.

"That's great! Well, this is me," the mayor said, walking up to a shiny new Corvette convertible that he had parked behind the cruiser. "Keep up the good work, my boy."

The mayor slapped Derek on the back again, then got in his car and drove off.

"Not your boy," Derek said to the retreating car.

He started wondering how Johann could afford such an expensive vehicle. He didn't think being the mayor of a small town paid that well.

It was obvious to Derek that the mayor was trying to distract him from what he was doing. Derek knew without a doubt old Johann was up to something. Derek went to his cruiser and climbed in. Maybe he needed to start keeping an eye on good old Mayor Johann.

Johann drove down the road a little way, then pulled over and picked up his phone. He dialed a number, waiting for someone to answer on the other end.

"Hey it's me," he said into the phone. "I'm going to be late. I was almost there when I ran into Deputy Capaldi poking around out in the woods. He was getting a little too close to your operation, so I had to lead him away."

He listened a beat, then responded, "No, I don't think he suspects anything. I could tell by the way he was answering my questions that he doesn't have a clue. Maybe he needs to be put on traffic duty for a while."

Johann chuckled then hung up.

Chapter Thirteen

I awoke the next morning with renewed purpose. Bart and I were going to start watching the cabin beginning today. I was going to find Gracie, no matter what I had to do. And I was going to get answers about this cabin one way or another.

I dressed in jeans, a tee shirt and sneakers and tied my hair back and pulled a baseball cap down over it. I put some water bottles and a few granola bars in my backpack, along with a pair of binoculars. This way I didn't have to get really close to the cabin in case the occupant showed up. For added protection, I threw in a can of pepper spray.

I called out to Bart who instantly appeared.

"Are you ready to do some surveillance?" I asked him.

"Yes ma'am. Let's go."

On the way to the creek, Bart was a non-stop chatterbox.

"This is so exciting, Miss Beth. I've never done anything like this. Oh, if my Loralee could see me now, she'd be so proud. What do you think we're going to find? Who do you think has been staying there? If they have Gracie and have hurt her in any way, I'll….well I'll….Pffft. I can't really do anything, now can I?"

I stopped to take a drink of water and said, "Bart, calm down. We are just going to watch the cabin and see if anyone shows up. There's no guarantee anyone will. For all we know that cabin has sat empty for years."

"You're right, Miss Beth. We don't know anything yet. I'm sorry, I just get so excited sometimes." (As evidenced by the trail of

M&Ms he was leaving.)

"Thank you for helping me, Bart. Loralee *would* be very proud of you right now."

I put the cap back on my water and we started off again. We made it to the creek, and I climbed the embankment to the trail leading into the woods.

"I just hope we can find that place again."

"Don't you worry none about that, Miss Beth. I only need to go someplace once, then the location is etched up here." Bart tapped one finger to the side of his head.

"We will have to find a good place to hide where we can still see the cabin, but where we can't be seen easily. At least I will," I amended.

Bart and I walked on until, once again, the woods got eerily quiet.

"I think we're getting close, Bart. Remember how quiet everything got just before we found the cabin?" I whispered.

"I sure do, Miss Beth. It was very spooky….and I'm a

ghost!" I chuckled softly.

Just then I caught a glimpse of the cabin.

"I think I see it, Bart."

Bart floated next to me as I tried to walk as quietly as I could. When I felt I had gotten close enough, I started searching around for a good hiding spot. I saw a cluster of bushes to my left and crept over to them. There was just enough room for me to scoot underneath. This spot gave me a terrific view of the front door of the cabin while keeping me hidden. I set my backpack down and dug out a bottled water and the binoculars. Now we wait.

Bart and I spoke in low tones to pass the time. I'd told him what Gracie and I had found in the library archives. He started talking about his and Loralee's families, what times were like in Raven's Glen when he lived here, and all the changes he'd witnessed here since his death.

We sat out there watching until midafternoon until I finally asked Bart if he was ready to go back home. It looked like it might rain. He agreed so I packed up my binoculars and now empty water bottles—I didn't want to leave any traces behind that we'd been here--and silently left the hiding spot.

When we got back to my house, Bart said, "I'm sorry we didn't have any luck today at that cabin, Miss Beth. But we can go again tomorrow if you'd like. We're sure to find something eventually."

"Sounds like a plan. Same time tomorrow?"

"You bet, Miss Beth. Just call to me when you're ready."

"Thank you, Bart, for all your help. I don't know what I'd do without you."

Bart's glow turned a bright pink. "I really haven't done much, ma'am."

"You've done more than you realize, Bart."

*****

Bart and I went back out into the woods the next day. We were talking quietly when I heard something.

"Bart! Do you hear that?"

Bart listened for a beat, then said, "I do, Miss Beth. Sounds like someone is walking through the woods toward the cabin." "And they aren't being very quiet about it either."

I picked my binoculars up and put them to my eyes. I zeroed in on the front door to the cabin.

Within minutes, A man came strolling up to the door. He didn't seem to be in any hurry, nor did he seem to be worried that someone might see him. He used a key, placed it in the front door lock, turned it, then opened the door and went inside.

"Bart!" I hissed. "Did you see who that man was?"

"He surely looked familiar, but I can't think of where I've seen him before."

"That was the mayor of Raven's Glen. Why would he be here and what does he have to do with all of this?"

"I don't reckon I know, Miss Beth, but it sure is getting stranger."

"We need to get back to the house and call Anna."

Within the hour, Bart and I were in my kitchen. I hadn't been taking my phone with me on these little excursions since I couldn't hold a good signal anyway. I picked it up from where it had been charging, unplugged it from said charger, and called Anna. It went to voicemail, so I left her a message to call as soon as she got this and hung up.

I needed to do something to occupy my time until I heard back from Anna. I sat down at the counter with paper and pen and started writing things down while it was still fresh in my mind. I didn't want to overlook anything when I told Anna what and who Bart and I had discovered.

Chapter Fourteen

Anna finally called back an hour or so later. Bart said he was going to pop out for a while.

"Beth, I am so sorry I missed your call. I had my phone on silent while I was meeting with a potential client. What's going on?"

I started telling Anna what Bart and I had been doing the past few days and what we'd found but was interrupted when the doorbell rang. "There's someone at the door. Hang on just a second, Anna."

I looked out the window and saw a police cruiser. Thinking there might be news about Gracie, I opened the door. Derek didn't look too glad to be there and even less so when I asked, "Any news?"

He walked into my living room without saying a word.

When he turned around, he looked at me. His amber eyes were cold. "Beth, where were you yesterday between the hours of one p.m. and five p.m.?"

"What?" I asked him, stunned.

"Answer the question, Ms. Woodson."

"I....I....I was here. At home."

"Can anyone verify and substantiate your claim, Ms. Woodson?"

"What's this about, Deputy Capaldi?"

"You are considered a person of interest and wanted for questioning in the disappearance of Mrs. Francesca Romano. I have strong reason to believe you and Jason Roberts were working together. Therefore, I have to take you down to the station. In addition to that, charges may be brought against you for impeding an investigation."

"What? I didn't do anything. I would never hurt Francesca. And what about Gracie? So, you're telling me Francesca is now missing and suggesting I had something to do with her disappearance as well?"

Anna started yelling through the phone, "Put me on speaker!" As soon as I did, she started yelling at Derek.

"Derek, I know you're working a lot and you're worn out. But you are not, I repeat, not going to arrest Beth. Have you lost your mind? I'm not sure what's gotten into you but knock it off!"

"This is official police business, Anna. Stay out of it."

"Sit tight, Beth. I'm on my way. And Derek, don't you move until I get there!"

Anna showed up within minutes. She squealed to a stop in the driveway next to Derek's cruiser, barged through the front door and walked straight up to her brother.

"If you think for one minute I'm going to stand by and let you arrest my friend, you are sadly mistaken. What do you have against Beth? She would never, I repeat, NEVER hurt Francesca. What is going on with you lately? And when did Francesca go missing? You know what? Never mind, I'll call Elsa."

I went to sit on the couch, and she walked over and sat down next to me.

She had just dialed Elsa when her brother asked, "Anna, why don't you ask your friend why I heard about her *husband* leaving town yesterday with her and her dog in the car?"

He pulled a small notebook out of his shirt pocket and flipped through it.

"Deputy Ahearn pulled one Jason Roberts over yesterday for speeding and reckless driving. He had a female companion with him who gave her name as Elizabeth Lynn Woodson and the dog's name as Gracie, when the deputy asked. She said she had just moved here and that I could verify that information as she didn't have any identification with her."

"The deputy was doing a visual search of the car and saw what turned out to be Francesca's purse with her wallet in the floorboard. The contents of both were scattered everywhere in the back. When asked, they claimed to have found it and were going to drop it off at the police station. They said they were looking through it to see if there was any identification. He told one of them to gather up the contents, then took the purse and wallet from them and let them go with a warning."

"When Elsa called in to tell us that Francesca was missing, that's when we started to suspect your little friend here was involved. A deputy will be coming by soon with a warrant to search the house. We haven't found her husband yet, but we have an APB and a warrant out for him to be brought in for questioning too."

"Jason is my ex-husband, and I was NOT with him.

Anna disconnected the call that had gone to Elsa's voicemail and pulled back from me.

"Is this true Beth? Are you playing a joke on us because if you are, it isn't funny."

"No Anna, I'm not. I would never let Gracie go anywhere with my exhusband. *I* wouldn't go anywhere with my ex-husband. I swear to you on my and Gracie's life, it wasn't me in that car. You think the mayor is disgusting? Get to know his doppelgänger by the name of Jason Roberts aka my ex-husband."

I kept throwing the 'ex' part in for Derek's benefit.

"Whomever you saw with my ex-husband, I assure you, wasn't me. My name isn't even Elizabeth. It's Beth—short for Bethany, not Elizabeth. I was here all day yesterday except when I went looking for Gracie in the woods. Bart can verify that information for you, unless you think he's in on the 'joke' too. Wait! Bart! Ask

Bart! He was with me. He will tell you he and I were together yesterday afternoon and today too. Ask him!" I called out for Bart, but he wasn't answering. I felt sick.

"Come on, Ms. Woodson. Don't make things harder on yourself."

Derek motioned for me to stand up. He informed me I could go in for questioning willingly or he could get a warrant. I looked at Anna, then Derek took my arm and led me out to his cruiser just as a second patrol car pulled up in front of my house and parked at the curb. The officer showed me the search warrant, then went into my house.

Anna jumped up off the couch, dropping her phone in the process.

"I'll be right down to get you out, Beth, just as soon as Deputy Hotshot finishes up here. Don't worry about a thing!"

To the other deputy, Anna said, "I promise, you won't find anything. My friend did not do this and I'm going to make sure you don't tear her house apart on the whims of my idiot brother!"

The deputy looked at Derek, who just shook his head.

Following us out of the house, Anna said to Derek, "I can't believe you! You and I are going to have a serious sit-down, little brother! Francesca is missing and you are here harassing Beth! Shame on you. Go out and find Francesca! Guiseppe must be worried sick!"

Derek ignored Anna, put me in the back of the cruiser and took me down to the police station. He sat me in an interrogation room until I could be questioned. I cannot believe this! To think that he would entertain the idea that I would cause harm to Francesca was beyond absurd!

I was sitting in a chair at a long table when I heard a commotion outside the door. I'd been here close to two hours at this point. I stood up and walked to the two-way mirror to see if I could figure out what was happening. I could hear several raised voices but couldn't see anything and couldn't make out what was being said.

Just then the door to the interrogation room opened and I heard Anna say, "We'll just see about that, won't we!"

Derek walked in followed by Anna and an older woman. Anna was holding on to the other woman's arm as they came toward where I was standing.

"See, Mama! See! He's treating my friend like a criminal. He doesn't have any other leads, so he's pinning it on Beth based on circumstantial evidence."

Anna and Derek's mom walked up to me. She was short in stature and pleasingly plump. She had dark hair with strands of gray woven in. She was dressed modestly head to toe in black and wearing sensible black low-heeled shoes.

She didn't say anything as she stared at me. She was looking at me like she was inspecting me from the inside out. She closed one eye and repeated the process. At least now I know where Derek gets his impenetrable stare from!

When she was finished, not before making me very uncomfortable from her scrutiny, she then turned to Derek and said, "Idiotata! You let poor girl go! She is pure of heart and mind."

Wow! Color me impressed.

"Mama..." Derek began.

Derek's mom slapped the back of his head.

"I say out! No back talk from you!"

Derek stepped aside to allow me to exit the room. Mrs. Capaldi then looped her arm through mine and she, Anna, and I walked to the lobby.

"Don't leave town, Ms. Woodson."

Mrs. Capaldi heard him and let go of my arm to turn and slap

Derek again.

"You no bother girl. Girl good! You find real bad guy. Bring Ms. Francesca and girl's doggy home!"

As we were walking away, Anna looked over her shoulder at Derek and stuck her tongue out at him.

"Yeah, sis. Real mature!"

The three of us left the sheriff's office and went to lunch. Mrs. Capaldi was a riot! She and my grandmother would get along fabulously. She spoke in broken English, sometimes a mix of English and Romanian if she couldn't find the right word to use in English.

"Beth, you should have seen the look on Derek's face when I walked into the office with Mama. Priceless!" she chuckled. "Mama is definitely better than any criminal lawyer, my husband aside," Anna said.

"I also followed Deputy Whats-his-name around while he was searching your house and made sure he put everything back the way he found it once he was finished searching. I wasn't about to stand by while he tossed the place then walked away, leaving it all for you to clean up afterwards."

"Let me guess, he didn't find anything either, did he?"

"Of course not!"

"Thanks for that, Anna!"

"What are friends for? I've got your back!"

"My son, he no smart sometimes. Head can be thick as brick," Mrs. Capaldi said while pointing to her head.

Anna and I laughed.

"Mama has the gift. She can look at a person and she just knows if they're good people or not. It's like she has a built-in soul scanner, and she can see it all."

I kept picturing a minicomputer in Mrs. Capaldi's eye that

scanned people from head to toe.

"I so sorry son is idiot," Mrs. Capaldi said.

"Oh, it's not your fault. It seems to be just the way my luck goes on this date," I replied.

"What's today?" Anna asked.

I sighed. "My birthday. Seems like the universe just can't give me this one day out of 365. My dog is missing, my ex-husband shows up in town with a woman claiming to be me, Francesca is missing, then I get hauled into jail to be questioned about said disappearance. This whole week has been so...."

"Oh, Beth! I'm so sorry. Happy birthday! We will all definitely go out for a girl's night to celebrate. Francesca and Gracie will be home in no time, you'll see!"

"I hope so, Anna."

Anna's mother reached over to me and engulfed me in a hug. I started tearing up.

Mrs. Capaldi released me, patted my back, then started telling us stories of her younger years as a little girl living in Romania. She spoke of the Great Uprising when a group of people decided "Loupe-garou were no good." This group started hunting lycanthropes, even though there had never been an issue with any of them, so Mrs. Capaldi's father packed up his family and moved them to London. People were a lot more accepting there. It was in London, while Mrs. Capaldi was at university, that she met Anna and Derek's father.

"Oh, he such a handsome gentleman. Always polite. Very caring."

They were married shortly after meeting, once both of them had graduated. Mr. Capaldi went to Mrs. Capaldi's dad beforehand and asked him for her hand. He readily agreed. It was many years later that Mr. and Mrs. Capaldi found out her husband's family was instrumental in assisting her fleeing family to get to safety. While both she and her husband were still children at the time her future in-laws helped and didn't know or remember, her father never forgot and was thrilled to give his dear friends' son his blessing.

"He was fine husband and father. Good provider and protector. No finer man ever lived."

Anna nodded her head in agreement. "Papa was truly a wonderful man."

"My boy has those qualities but he get stubborn like jackass. Gets on high horse. I have to knock him down a few pegs sometimes. Make him see he not always right. But he a good man!"

I began telling Anna and her mother about my grandmother and the crazy things she gets into sometimes.

"My mother is as normal as can be. My grandmother though!"

"I would love to meet grandmother. She sound like fun person!"

I couldn't imagine Anna's sensible mother hanging out with my grandmother. That would definitely be interesting!

It was then our waiter brought out a cupcake with a single candle in it. The wait staff sang happy birthday to me as Anna and her mother smiled.

"We had to do a little something, Beth," Anna said.

I thanked both Anna and her mother, then remembered I had news.

"Oh, Anna, before I forget again. I was calling you earlier to tell you something before I was hauled off to the pokey."

"That's right! What was your news?"

"Well, Bart and I have been out looking in the woods for Gracie. We found a footprint right around the area where she was taken. Bart and I started searching the woods and we came upon an abandoned looking cabin way deep in the woods. We almost missed it. We noticed some things inside when we peeked in the windows. It gives the appearance of being abandoned, but we think someone is staying there."

"Do you remember me telling you when Gracie was taken that when Bart started to follow, he felt like he'd been frozen in place? I found an empty metal canister on the ground where Bart said it happened. It's in my backpack at home. And that's not the best part!"

"Don't keep me in suspense!" Anna exclaimed.

"Well, we decided to do a little surveillance on the place and went out the last few days to watch. We found a nice little hiding spot where we were close enough to watch but hidden so we couldn't be seen."

"Beth, please tell me you didn't go inside the cabin. Do you know the danger you put yourself in?"

"We were fine, Anna, and, no, I didn't go inside. Bart and I were hiding in some bushes near the front of the cabin."

"We had gone out today and just when we were ready to give up and consider it a lost cause, a man showed up and went in. You will never guess who it was!"

"Who? Tell me!"

"Our one and only Mayor Johann Wilson!"

"What? What was he doing way out there? As far as I know, he doesn't own property there."

"I don't know but once we were sure he was inside, we snuck out of there as quick as we could. I came straight home to call you. With the ensuing chaos, it slipped my mind, but when I was sitting in that room, waiting to be questioned, I started thinking. I had planned to tell Derek this when he questioned me, but never got the chance. Do you think the mayor is involved in all of this?"

"Girl, you're going to give me a heart attack! That is strange that Johann would be way out there in the middle of nowhere. I'm going to run you and Mama home, then I'll come back to my office. I'll get on my computer and pull some property records and a plat map of the town. That should show who owns that cabin. I'll call you when I find out. Don't go back out there, please Beth. Promise me you'll stay away. If Johann is involved, you don't want him to know you've seen him sneaking around. He may be an oaf, but lord knows what he's capable of if you've caught him getting up to no good."

"Yes, dear girl," Anna's mother said. "Keep distance. Let brick head son take from here."

"Ok. I promise to stay away."

We stood up to leave the diner. Anna would take her mother home, then drop me off to do her research.

When we dropped Anna's mother off, I got out of the back and walked up to get in the front seat. Anna hugged her mother and kissed her cheek. Mrs. Capaldi walked up to me and cupped her hand, placing it on my cheek and patting it a few times.

"Very nice to meet you, Beth. You will have to bring grandmother to visit me. We let our hair down, kick off shoes, and have a big time."

Unfortunately, I wasn't sure if Grams would stop at just taking her shoes off.

"I will definitely bring her around, Mrs. Capaldi. It was very nice meeting you as well."

"Bye Mama. I will call you later."

Anna and I got back into her SUV, and she took me home.

"I'll call you as soon as I find out something," she told me as I was getting out of her car. "Sit tight. It shouldn't take long."

Within an hour, Anna called me back.

"I've pulled all the property records and I'm not coming up with anything. There is no owner on record for this cabin. The property doesn't show up in any search."

"Do you have any ideas as to why? I mean, there's obviously a cabin there. Can anyone just build a structure wherever they want without registering as the owner?"

"No. Each and every piece of property, regardless of age and condition has to be registered if someone buys it. Even if it's just an empty plot or a patch of woods. No one can just build a structure on land they don't own. What is that idiot up to?"

"Not sure but he walked in like he owned the place. He didn't seem too worried about getting caught either."

"Hmmmmm. I'm going to try to get in touch with Derek. He's still pouting, but I know how to get him to cave. I'll keep you posted."

"Sounds good, Anna."

"And Beth?"

"Yes?"

"You've done enough. Stay out of those woods from here on out."

"Yes, Mother."

"I'm serious. We don't know what we're dealing with. Please! Stay out. Let Derek take it from here."

"Okay, Anna, but if Derek doesn't find something out, I'm going back. I just know Gracie and Francesca are in that cabin somewhere. I feel it in my bones!"

Chapter Fifteen

Bart decided to be brave for one of the few times in his life. The last two days, after he'd been in the woods with Beth, he'd been leaving the house without telling her and going back to the cabin in the woods to keep watch. Beth had done so much for him so maybe he could return some of her kindness and find Gracie. He and Gracie were rapidly becoming friends and he missed her.

Today he saw the mayor coming back again. He opened the door and went inside for a little while, then came out with another man. Wait! The man he was with was the one who took Gracie!

Bart's aura started glowing a dark red; so dark it was almost black. He thought about following those two but decided to wait it out. One or both of them would be back, he was sure of it!

He wasn't disappointed. About an hour later, both men came back, and the mayor had a woman slung over his shoulder, carrying her inside. The other man was leading the way.

Bart could hear snippets of their conversation and what he heard made him even more mad!

"Walter, are you sure this is a good idea? She's pretty well known in town."

"Just shut up and bring her in, Johann. I don't care how popular she is. She's friends with that nosy human girl. That girl should have minded her own business. You'd think when we took her dog, she would have stopped poking around, but no! Besides, I haven't had a vampire to study yet. Now, let's get her in, get the collar on her before she wakes up, and get her in the cage."

"She's heavy. Why do I have to do all the heavy lifting?"

"These hands belong to science. They weren't made for manual labor. Now stop complaining and get her in. You're getting paid a hefty fee for bringing me these monsters, so earn your money, you whining imbecile."

They disappeared into the depths of the cabin.

"Oh no!" Bart exclaimed to himself. "I think they have Francesca!"

Torn between going back to tell Beth and trying to find a way into the cabin, Bart went with the latter. He flew to the structure and tried to float through the door. He was instantly thrown backwards. Next, he tried the only three windows in the cabin with the same result. Lastly, he tried just floating through the wall. Still no luck.

"What in blue blazes is blocking me. Why can't I get in?" Bart said to himself.

Finally admitting defeat, he started back to tell Beth.

When he got back to the house, he called out for Beth before just appearing, although with the news he had, he was sure she'd forgive him if he did just pop in. But a deal is a deal. There was no answer. He appeared fully, going from room to room, calling out for Beth as he went.

"Now where the dickens did she get off to?" he asked the empty house.

Not finding her, he returned to the kitchen. He thought he'd hang around for a bit to wait for her. Surely, she wouldn't be gone that long. After waiting a couple of hours, he started to get worried, especially when he noticed Beth had left her empty coffee mug in the sink. She usually rinsed it out once they returned from their surveillance. Plus, he noticed her purse was on the counter and her cell phone was sitting next to her purse.

She wouldn't leave the house without either of those. That was so not like her. Something must have happened. Something bad!

Bart thought about what to do. He really needed to tell Beth about what he'd found and tell her they had Francesca. She could call Anna and have Anna get Derek involved. But now it looked like something had happened to Beth. He wasn't sure who else to turn to, so he decided to go back out and keep an eye on the cabin.

*****

I went to the kitchen when I awoke the next morning for coffee. I poured myself a cup, grabbed a pastry, and started to sit down at the table when I noticed a paper on the floor in front of the back door. I walked over to see what it was.

In all manners of cliché, someone cut letters out of the newspaper and glued them to a blank white sheet of paper. The note read:

'Back off if you ever want to see your friends again!'

Taped below the letters on the same paper was a picture of Gracie. She was in a cage with what looked like a homemade shock collar on. Her fur was dirty and matted and her eyes looked glassy. There was also a second picture. It was Francesca! In the picture, she was in a cage too with the same kind of collar around her neck.

Oh my God! I called out to Bart. Strange! He wasn't responding. I called Anna. These people had gone too far now.

"Good morning, Beth. I'm afraid I don't have any news. I didn't hear from my brother the rest of the day yesterday and he isn't returning my texts."

"Anna..." I broke off sobbing.

"Beth? Beth! What's wrong? What's happened? Have they found Gracie?"

"No!" I wailed. "There...there...there was a note that someone slid under my door last night. It had a picture of Gracie along with...." I started sobbing so hard, I couldn't speak.

"Beth! Honey, talk to me. Along with what?"

"Oh, Anna! There was a horrible picture of Francesca! And now Bart is missing too!"

"What?!? I'm dropping the kids off at school and then I'm on my way over."

Anna screeched to a stop in my driveway twenty minutes later. I was sitting in a chair on the front porch.

"Alright Beth. Let me see it."

I showed her the note and pictures. Those pictures broke my heart into a million pieces. Just wait until I find the person responsible!

"I'm calling Derek."

Anna dialed her brother's number, but the call went to voicemail.

"Derek Michael Capaldi, stop this nonsense right now. You need to get over to Beth's house as soon as you get this. I will not stand for someone threatening and tormenting my friends. If you aren't here soon, I'll call Mom." Anna hung up.

"That always gets him. He hates it when our mom gets angry at him, especially when he's being pig headed."

Anna and I went inside and went into the kitchen for coffee. Anna happened to walk over and look out the back door.

"Beth, what happened to your car?"

I walked over next to Anna and looked out where I had parked my car in the back. Someone had slashed my tires, broken the windshield wipers, smashed the headlights and taillights and shattered the windows. They'd also dumped what looked like red paint all over it.

"What the crap?" I gasped.

Anna was grabbing her phone just as we heard a car pull up out front. We both went back to the living room and looked out the window to see who was there.

A police cruiser pulled up in front of my house and a uniformed Derek got out. He did not look happy. I sincerely hoped this wasn't going to be a repeat of yesterday.

Anna opened the door for him before he could even ring the bell.

"Okay, Anna. What kind of drama is your friend dragging you into now? I don't have time for this. I have missing people on my hands right now."

"Beth, show him the note."

I handed the note to Derek. He swore then asked, "Where and when did you find this?"

"It was on my kitchen floor this morning when I got up. I guess someone slid it under the back door."

"And" Anna added, "take a look at what they did to her car."

"What? What happened to your car?"

"Someone really did a number on it, Derek," Anna said.

Derek went into the kitchen, went out the back door and started checking out the damage to my car. When he came back in, concern was written all over his face. He looked at the note I'd received again.

"Okay, let's start at the beginning."

I told him how I'd found the note on the floor this morning and how it looked like someone had slid it under the door. Anna picked up the story, telling Derek about seeing my car.

"Bart and I found something in the woods that's maybe worth checking out again. Especially since the sheriff's office seems to think I'm up to all sorts of nefarious misdeeds. And, speaking of Bart, I haven't seen him since yesterday. I'm starting to get worried."

"You shouldn't be out in those woods by yourself Ms. Woodson. You don't know who or what could be lurking around," Derek said, thinking about the mayor.

"Ohhhh *now* you're concerned. Wouldn't it be better for you, and probably the town too, if I disappeared like the others? Oh wait. That would probably make me look even more guilty, wouldn't it? You said you weren't going to look for Gracie anymore. You had 'real cases' to work on. Fine! Go work on your real cases. I'm going to find my dog and my friends!"

Derek looked briefly ashamed then said, "Ms. Woodson. Beth. Stop. I'm sorry I accused you of wrongdoing. I was just doing my job, based on evidence that was presented to me. Obviously, this note, and your car were warnings. You're on someone's radar. Let me do my job. This town is my responsibility. Stay out of the investigation before the threats become more than that."

"I'm letting you do your job. And I'm taking care of my dog who is my responsibility."

"Ok you two, enough!" Anna said, stepping between us. "I swear, you're both stubborn and hard-headed and you're at an impasse. Just stop! Beth, please tell Derek what you and Bart found. Think of Francesca and Gracie. What they are going through. Maybe it will help Derek find them."

I looked at Anna, but the look on her face left no room for argument.

"Fine!"

I proceeded to tell him about the cabin Bart and I found and how it looked as though someone was using it, even though it looked abandoned. I told him about Bart and I staking out the cabin and how the mayor had shown up.

Derek swore.

"I was all over those woods, and I didn't see a cabin. I didn't even pick up a scent. I'm inclined to agree with you, Ms. Woodson. Someone is using that cabin but covering their tracks quite well.

That explains why I ran into Johann when I was out there the other day. I knew he was up to something by the way he was acting. Why didn't you tell me this sooner?"

"Well, gee, officer, let's see. Hmmmm.....I've been just a little busy being accused of things I had nothing to do with, taken to jail, having my house searched. If you would have listened to me for five seconds instead of thinking the worst of me, I might have been able to tell you."

"Tell me where you found it."

"Why don't I show you?"

"Ms. Woodson, this is part of an official investigation. I can't have you inserting yourself in the middle of it, nor can I endanger your safety by allowing you to go."

"Well then I guess I really don't remember."

"Don't be stubborn. I can always ask Bart."

"If you can find him. I can't get a hold of him. For all I know, they've taken him too." I stared at Derek, unblinking.

"Look, do you want to find your dog? What about Francesca? Just tell me. Lives are at stake, and I don't have time for games."

"Please, Beth," Anna begged. "Do it for Gracie and Francesca."

I turned to Derek and said "Go to the creek bed. It's up the bank and to the right. But it's way back in the woods. You'll never find it. Please let me go with you."

"I'll find it Ms. Woodson. Stay here with my sister. I'll send her updates."

Bart suddenly appeared, startling Beth, Anna, and Derek.

"Officer Capaldi, Miss Beth, Miss Anna," Bart said, glowing a beautiful blue color. "I'm so glad I've finally found you. I have news!"

"Bart! Where have you been? I've been worried about you. I called out several times, but you never responded."

"I've been looking for you as well and I was fearing the worst. Especially after what I've found. Where did you get off to?"

I looked at Derek, then said, "It's a long story. So, what did you find?" "I've been going back out to that cabin, just to keep an eye on things. I was hoping to find Gracie and bring her home. After all you've done for me, I figured it was the least I could do."

"Anyway, nothing was really happening until yesterday. I was in our usual stakeout spot when that mayor fellow showed up. He went inside, then came back out with the man who took Gracie! They left together and I was going to follow them but decided to wait and see what happened."

"Soon the both of them came back and Johann had a woman he was carrying slung over his shoulder. I couldn't believe it when I saw it was Francesca! I tried to get inside the cabin, but for some reason I was blocked."

"That's when I came back here to tell you, but I couldn't find you. I was plenty scared that they took you too. I've been out there watching all last night and today. It's been quiet. The mayor left but that man was still there."

We listened to Bart's discovery, then Derek said, I'm going out there." "I'm going with you," I told Derek.

"No, Beth. Stay here with my sister. It's too dangerous. I'm trained for situations like this."

"Officer Capaldi, May I go with you? I can show you the way," Bart asked.

"Sure Bart. Let's go."

Derek and Bart went out the back door as I stood glaring at their backs.

"Traitor," I mumbled at Bart's back.

Chapter Sixteen

Anna and I sat around the house waiting to hear something from Derek. Anna had tried calling Francesca and Elsa's phones to see if what we'd heard was true, but they went straight to voicemail.

Anna's phone rang and she answered on the first ring.

"Hello? Derek?"

She looked at me and mouthed, "It's Elsa," then put the call on speaker.

"Elsa, I'm at Beth's. We've been so worried about you. What happened? I've been calling, but it keeps going to voicemail."

Elsa told us all she knew about the day Francesca disappeared. We told her what we had found and told her Derek was out searching as we were speaking.

"Frank won't let me leave the house. He's worried something will happen to me. This is just so terrible. I should have never left Francesca alone."

"Honey, it's not your fault! Please don't blame yourself. My brother will find her, you'll see."

We spoke a few minutes longer, then disconnected, assuring Elsa we would keep her updated as we got news.

Derek had been gone for about two hours. True to his word, he texted Anna with updates.

About a half hour after the last text from Derek, Anna's phone rang.

"Hi, Derek. Any news?" she asked hopefully.

She listened for a few seconds, then a strange look came over her.

"Hello? Derek? Answer me! Hello?"

"What's wrong, Anna?" I asked.

"That was strange. Derek said he had found the cabin and he was going to see if he could get in and take a look around. Then I heard a scuffle, Derek was yelling, and the line went dead."

Bart appeared in the kitchen at that moment, glowing bright red and looking like he was out of breath.

"Miss Anna! Miss Beth! You have to help!"

"Bart, what happened?"

Bart was gulping in air, M&Ms pouring out behind him.

"Derek and I were at the cabin. Derek was walking around, trying to find a way in. Out of nowhere, this man jumped out and pounced on him. They started fighting, then the man stuck Derek with a needle, and Derek passed out."

"The man dragged him in the cabin. I tried to get in, but I was blocked somehow. I looked in the windows and saw the man dragging Derek across the room, then he disappeared around a corner, and I couldn't see anymore."

"I don't know if that man knew I was there or not. If he did, he paid me no never mind. We have to help Derek. I don't know what that man has planned for him but I'm sure it isn't good!"

"Oh my God! My brother! I'm calling Jerry. He'll know what to do," said Anna as she started dialing her husband.

They spoke on the phone for a few minutes while she filled him in. When she hung up, she told me, "Jerry is picking the kids up from school and taking them to my mom's, then he's on his way. He's going to call Frank and Giuseppe too." She started to cry. "If anything happens to Derek, I don't know what I'll do."

"Anna, I won't stand by and do nothing. This is my fault. I should have insisted on going with him. I know exactly where the cabin is. I'm going out there."

"Beth, no! You don't know what or who is out there. And if this man can overpower my brother, God only knows what he'll do to you. Wait for the men. Please! I don't want something to happen to you too."

"No. Derek is out there, and I just know Francesca and Gracie are too. Bart can take the men to the cabin. There's no time to waste. I'm going. I'll call you with any news."

I grabbed my cell phone, stuck it in my pocket and ran out the back door. I couldn't figure out how Derek could get service out there on his phone when mine was spotty at best. I'd take it anyway just in case.

******

The man in the cabin opened a trap door in the floor. He knew when he put the trapdoor in, he'd done an excellent job. Unless you knew it was there, you'd never notice it.

He dragged Derek to the opening, then rolled him down the steps into the basement the man had turned into a laboratory. He dragged Derek over to an empty cage, pushed him in, then shut and locked the door, but not before snapping a collar in place around Derek's neck. Where was that idiot Johann when he needed him? He shouldn't have to risk his hands doing the heavy lifting.

He chuckled to himself as he said, "Haven't had a werewolf yet. This will be a nice addition to study."

Gracie sat in another cage. "I don't know who you are or what you've been doing, but you won't get away with it much longer. My human is looking for me and you can be sure Derek's disappearance is going to bring a world of trouble to your doorstep!"

"Hush, you abomination! No one has found me yet and no one will." Another man walked in whistling until he noticed Derek in a cage.

"What the hell, Walter? What are you doing with Derek Capaldi? Do you know how much trouble you've just opened us up to?"

"Shut up Johann. He's sleeping like a baby. And even when he does wake up, he can't do a thing. How he ever found this place is beyond me, but if I were a betting man, I'd say that meddling girl led him here. If she shows up, I may have a little surprise for her too!"

Walter rubbed his hands together and cackled with maniacal glee.

"You'd better not hurt Beth, you monster," Gracie growled. "If you do, I'll make sure you pay for it dearly."

"Didn't I just tell you to be quiet?" Walter held up a remote, waving it around. He pressed a button and Gracie yelped, cowering in the back of her cage.

"Guess you needed a little reminder that I'm in charge here, not you!" Walter said, dropping the remote back into his lab coat pocket.

"I didn't sign on for this, Walter! Ghosts, talking dogs, witches, leprechauns, that's one thing. But now you've taken a deputy? You're getting careless, Walter. You're taking too many risks, starting with the vampire. Oh no! I'm out of here. I'm not going down for this," Johann said.

Johann turned to leave, but Walter was on him before he could reach the stairs. He pulled a hypodermic needle from his coat pocket and stuck Johann in the neck. Johann dropped to the floor.

"Why not? Let's add a troll to my collection," Walter said with hysterical glee as he dragged Johann to another empty cage.

Chapter Seventeen

I ran through the woods as fast as I could while trying to avoid falling on the uneven ground or tripping over an exposed root. When I got close to the cabin, I pulled out my cell phone and called Anna. Amazingly enough, I had just enough of a signal to call.

"It's me. I'm almost at the cabin. I can see it. Have the guys gotten there yet?"

"Jerry just got here. He called Frank and Guiseppe who are pulling up now."

"Okay. Have Bart lead them here. I'm going in."

"Beth no! Wait for them."

"No time, Anna. Gotta…." The call dropped.

I put the phone on silent, just in case, and slid it into my back pocket. I cautiously approached the cabin, trying to avoid crunching on the vegetation or stepping on twigs. I didn't want to announce my arrival too soon. I noticed a phone that I assumed to be Derek's laying in the dirt outside the cabin door. The screen was shattered, looking as though someone had stepped on it repeatedly.

I stepped up to the side and looked in the window, keeping an ear out for anyone trying to sneak up on me. I didn't see anything, so I went around to the front.

I tried the front door and was shocked when it opened. I pushed it open as quietly as I could but didn't bother to shut it in case I needed to make a hasty retreat.

I walked as quietly as I could through the cabin. When I got to the kitchen, I thought I heard someone singing. I stopped where I was and listened to figure out where the singing was coming from. It sounded like it was coming from below, but I didn't see a door or any way to get down there.

I tiptoed around to the kitchen and then noticed in the corner a piece of flooring that wasn't sitting right. Just about the time I started to check it out, I heard footsteps coming up.

I quickly and quietly made my way back to the living room and slid between the headboard of the bed and the wall. I could see just a little through the boards on the headboard and saw a man walk around the corner, whistling.

He walked to the front door, noticed it open and said, "Idiot Johann. Don't you know how to close doors? And you're worried *I'm* going to get us caught? Ha!"

He went out the door, closing it behind him.

I waited a few beats, then came out of my hiding space. I ran back into the kitchen and saw the piece of flooring was now flush with the rest of the floor. I went through the kitchen drawers and found a butter knife.

I dug the knife down into the flooring groove and managed to pry the piece away. There was a set of stairs leading down. I set the flooring aside and went down.

The space opened up into some sort of laboratory. Cages lined both sides of the walls and, out of eight, only one was empty. I looked in each one as I passed. It seemed everyone was wearing a shock collar with the exception of whoever or whatever was in the very last cage. It appeared to be a big black shadow. The first cage was empty, but the second held a man dressed in a green shirt and a tartan plaid kilt. He eyed me up and down but said nothing. The third one held someone, but I wasn't sure who since they were laying on their side in the back of the cage, facing the wall. I saw Gracie in the last cage next to this one wearing the shock collar she had on in the picture.

"Beth! Oh Beth, be careful. If that man comes back, I don't know what he'll do to you!"

I ran down to Gracie's cage to let her out. Unfortunately, there were padlocks on all the doors.

"Gracie girl! I have missed you so much! What happened? How am I going to get you out of here?"

"Beth don't worry about me. You need to watch for that man. I don't know where he went, but he's never gone long."

I crossed to the other side but didn't stop at the last cage on this side of the room since I wasn't sure what it held. Francesca was in the next cage diagonally across the room from Gracie. There was an older woman caged next to her. Both Francesca and the old woman were wearing shock collars, but the old woman had some sort of strange symbols written on the floor outside of her cage. I saw Johann was in the first cage on this side, but I ran back to Francesca's cage while the old woman watched me with curiosity.

"Beth, what are you doing here? Listen to Gracie. Leave and go get help before he comes back."

"How did you get here?" I asked her.

"Elsa and I had gone to an art exhibit and were leaving the gallery. I stopped to go to the ladies' room and Elsa went out to get the car. When I came out of the ladies' room, I felt what I thought was a mosquito bite me on the neck. That's all I remember until I woke up in here."

"He came back a while ago, dragging some other poor soul in. From back here, I couldn't see who. He's in the cage next to Gracie. Then Johann came in, they got into an argument, and he ended up putting Johann in a cage too. Apparently, they're working together. I knew Johann was a slime ball. This just proves it," added Francesca.

I crossed back over, looked in the cage next to Gracie's and saw Derek. He was just starting to come around, wearing his own shock collar.

"Derek! Are you okay? Hold on. I'm going to try to figure out how to get you all out of here."

Derek looked at me and said, "Beth! What are you doing here? Are you trying to get yourself killed? You need to get out of here. Go get help."

"Help is on the way but I'm here and I'm going to try to get you out."

I pulled my cell phone out and saw I had no service here in the basement. Figures! Technology works anywhere in the world except for when and where you need it the most!

I started searching through the desk, file drawers, anywhere I thought there might be keys for the locks.

"Beth, it's no use. He keeps the keys to these locks with him. Gracie's right. Go get help before he comes back. He's crazy and I don't want to see you get hurt. He took my gun. Not sure what he did with it."

"It's fine. Just let me think."

Then I heard the front door to the cabin open. "Oh crap. What am I going to do? I need to hide!" "Beth!" Derek hissed.

I shushed Derek and ran around looking for a place to hide. There was a space between the wall and one of the filing cabinets in the back. I squeezed back there and tried to calm my breathing as the man came down the steps.

Chapter Eighteen

"Come out, come out, wherever you are. I have a present for you. I see you've found my little playroom. If you come out, you can play too."

He started walking around the room, searching under tables, the desk, anywhere he thought someone could be hiding.

"Aww, I see you're scared. There's nothing to be scared of. Come on out. We'll have a nice conversation. I'll fill you in on what I'm doing here. Who knows? Maybe you can become my new assistant. Seems my last one didn't work out so well."

A groggy voice came from the opposite side of the room from Derek and Gracie.

"It's that Woodson woman, Walter. She came in after you left, snooping around. Found her dog and her boyfriend over there."

"Shut up Johann," Derek yelled.

"What are you going to do about it? You're not such a big bad werewolf now, are you?"

"When I get out of here, you're going to pay, you slimy bridge dweller. I can't believe you're involved in this."

Derek charged the cage but was rewarded with a shock from his collar that knocked him back. Johann laughed.

"Johann, we all knew you were a slimy, pompous, egotistical jerk, but I never figured you to be a heartless brute," said Francesca.

Johann ignored her.

"Come on, Walter. I'm sorry about earlier. I just panicked when I saw the werewolf. Let me out and we can pick up where we left off. No hard feelings!"

Walter chuckled and replied, "Not on your life. I rather like the idea of having a troll to study again."

Walter started walking around the lab, searching for Beth.

"Well, now that I know who our guest is, won't you please come out? We can get acquainted. Sit down and talk over a cup of tea. Wouldn't that be nice?"

"Walter, she's behind that cabinet in the back," supplied Johann. "Let me out so I can join the party."

Derek growled, "Johann, when I get out of here, I'm going to tear you apart. Do you hear me?"

"Oooh! The big bad wolf comes out. He huffs and he puffs but can't blow his cage down!" Again, Johann started laughing hysterically at his own joke.

Walter walked back to the cabinet I was hiding behind. I had nowhere to go.

"Ahhh there you are, Ms. Woodson. Please come out. I promise I won't hurt you."

Yeah! Like I was going to believe anything that came out of his mouth!

I slid out of my hiding place and faced the madman standing in front of me.

"Who are you and why do you have my dog and these people in here? What are you doing with them? And why have you been following me? Everywhere I went, you were there."

"Uh, uh, uh, Ms. Woodson. First, we must have a proper round of introductions. There will be a question-and-answer segment later. This way please. And, oh, don't try anything foolish. I'd hate to see something happen to your dog. Gracie, is it?"

He pulled a remote control out of his pocket and pressed a button. Gracie howled in pain.

"Don't hurt my dog. I'll do whatever you want, but don't hurt her. Do you hear me?"

"Ms. Woodson, that was just a tiny shock. Imagine what would happen if I were to increase the voltage. I have the upper hand here. You are in no position to issue threats. Now, come, have a seat."

We walked over to his desk, and he pulled up a second chair. He sat in one and motioned for me to take the other.

"I'll stand, thanks."

"That wasn't an invitation. Sit! Now! Before you really start to annoy me."

He pulled the remote from his pocket again.

I looked at Gracie and Derek, then back at Walter. I sat down.

"Fine! I'm sitting. Now what do you want? Why do you have my dog and the others here? What are you doing to them?"

"In good time, my dear."

He picked up a teapot from a hot plate on top of the desk. He poured himself some into a mug, then offered me some. I shook my head and he put the teapot back on the hot plate.

"Ms. Woodson, my name is Walter Frankenstein. Dr. Walter Frankenstein. I'm a scientist and a creator. I'm sure you've had the pleasure of meeting two of my most successful creations—Elsa and Frank Stein? Frank, you see, was trial and error. I had all the parts, I had the know-how to put them together, I just wasn't sure *how* to join them. There were several others before Frank, but they kept losing body parts here, body parts there. I had to destroy each of them and start over. When I got to Frank, I had the brilliant idea to try Velcro. And it worked! Finally! I had created a living, breathing masterpiece. The only drawback was you could see the Velcro. But the Velcro held.

Frank didn't lose his head over silly things!"

The doctor laughed maniacally before continuing.

"I educated Frank. I taught him how to walk, speak, then read and write. I educated him in the classics—music, books, movies! He was intelligent and picked up on things quickly. I still didn't like the Velcro, but he was so bright that I didn't have the heart to destroy him. Destroying him would have been like killing my own child. And he kind of was."

"While Frank studied every day, I went back to thinking of ways I could create another being, only without the visible attachments. Frank needed a companion and I needed to perfect my craft. One day, it just came to me. Undertaker's thread! How silly of me to have never thought about that one beautiful solution to a problem that had eluded me for so long. And then along came Elsa. Oh, she was so beautiful! I picked only the best and most perfect parts for her. She was by far, my most successful creation."

He looked over at the cage Francesca was being held in, watching him spin his tale of insanity. He pushed a different button on the remote and gave her a small shock. Francesca covered her face with her hands and started sobbing.

I felt my blood pressure rising and it took everything in me not to pounce on this lunatic.

"I worked with her every day tirelessly as I had Frank. She, too, was a quick study. When I felt she was ready, I decided to introduce her to Frank. The first meeting wasn't quite the success I'd hoped it would be. Frank was curious, but Elsa was terrified! I tried without success every day until finally I decided enough was enough. I put them in the same room together, but I couldn't have them roaming about freely, taking the chance they'd do harm or destroy each other. I put them in cages like the ones you see here. It took some time, but finally they came together in acceptance of one another."

"The three of us became one big, happy family, or so I thought. We were together every day, studying, learning. We dined together, went to museums, art fairs, you name it. By now I could trust the two of them together without fear of mishaps. They were getting along beautifully. A bit too beautifully, as it turned out."

"One day, I stepped out alone to go into the city. I was picking up some tickets at the box office for Swan Lake for the three of us as a surprise. Imagine *my* surprise when I came back home and found the two of them gone. Vanished! I felt so hurt. Betrayed. My family, the one I had created, had left me."

"I searched for years and one day, I ran upon this town. Best of all, I had found my Frank and Elsa! The only problem was, there were other monsters here of various types and breeds, and they seemed to have all banded together. I built this cabin and decided to watch and wait for my chance. When the opportunity presented itself, I would take back my family and leave. That was my plan initially."

While the doctor was telling his story, I'd glance around from time to time and look at the other caged beings. Derek, Gracie, and the rest of them all sat quietly, listening with rapt attention. He continued.

"While awaiting my chance, I started wondering about all the creatures in this town. And, oh, what a variety! As far as I can tell from following you, you're the only human resident of permanency besides myself,
that is," he chuckled. "Aren't you just a little bit afraid to be living among monsters? These immoral, bloodthirsty creatures?"

Monsters? Really? Hello pot, meet kettle.

"I decided I would like to stop creating beings and begin to study them. See if I could figure out how their magic worked. What gave them their superpowers, if you will, and what disabled them. So, I began taking wayward creatures I'd run across that I thought no one would miss. I had a plethora of choices right at my fingertips!"

"The first was a little ghost girl in a wedding dress. I was out walking in the woods one day when I happened upon her. She told me she'd been in an accident and asked me if I'd seen her fiancé. I'd told her no, but I would be happy to help her look. She was walking along beside me as I pretended to look. I pointed to the cabin and told her I thought I'd seen someone go inside. Maybe it was her fiancé. The poor trusting girl!"

"She followed me right in and down the stairs to the lab. I managed to trick her into getting in the cage. She's the only one a shock collar wouldn't work on, being incorporeal, so I had to improvise. I made a ring around the iron cage with sea salt imported from the Dead Sea and also wiped the bars of the cage with it. She was trapped! I'd done it! Oh, she cried and begged me to free her, but I couldn't, you see. I couldn't take the chance that she'd leave, then tell someone about this place. Not when I was just getting started!"

"I've tried different experiments with her over the years. Some successful, some not so much. At some point, she quit talking and stopped begging me to set her free. It's almost as though she became resigned to her fate. It was time to find another."

I looked over in a cage on the far back of the wall and there was Loralee! She was surrounded by a thick black glow, which is why I didn't notice her initially. She almost looked like a shadow. I was getting angrier by the minute, but knew I had to keep a clear head and just bide my time.

"While searching for my next subject, I found Johann. He was lying under the bridge by the lake. He'd been beaten up pretty badly and was covered in blood, mud, you name it."

"Stupid goats got the jump on me," Johann supplied.

Walter looked at him and shook his head, then went back to his story.

"Anywho.... I wasn't sure what kind of creature he was, but I came back here, got my wagon, and went back to where I'd found him. He was near death, and I wasn't sure if he'd even make it back here without succumbing to his injuries."

"I brought him inside, cleaned him up, and tended to his wounds. He'd lost a substantial amount of blood from all of his injuries, so I ended up giving him transfusions of my own blood in a last-ditch effort to save him. I wasn't sure what effect human blood would have on him, but it was worth a try to find out. If it didn't work, I'd just replace him with another being. There were plenty of choices here, you see." Walter stopped talking to take a sip of his tea.

"Don't get me wrong, I still wasn't sure what he was, so I kept him locked in a cage between treatments, as well as placing a shock collar around his neck. One can never be too careful when dealing with monsters and I had to take every precaution available to me in order to protect myself."

"One day I came back from one of my search missions and I noticed Johann was sitting up in his cage. He was still looking quite poorly, but he was awake. I'd done it! I'd saved him from near death! I made him a bowl of chicken noodle soup and, oh, how he sucked it down. I cautioned him to go slow and started asking him questions."

"Every day I tended to him, and he got better, stronger. He'd told me his name and as much as he could remember about the horrible attack on him. When I'd asked what he was, he'd told me he was a troll. Imagine! I'd infused my own human blood into a troll, and he survived without any side effects. I decided right then and there, my blood, my very life force had magical healing properties."

Yeah, don't break your arm patting yourself on the back, you lunatic!

"When Johann had fully recovered, he asked me about my laboratory and took interest in what I was doing. At this point,

I was starting to trust him. We'd spent so much time together and he had my blood running through his veins, so I explained to him about my experiments. He volunteered to help me. He was familiar with most of the monsters here and he could help me capture some. I readily agreed. After all, I'm not cut out for heavy labor. I made a deal with him that for every being he brought to me when I needed another, he would be paid a substantial reward."

"Johann was the one who brought the witch in. He went to visit her under the premise of needing an herbal potion to help with arthritis. As she turned her back and started mixing up his remedy, he snuck up behind her and placed a cloth coated with ether that I'd given him over her face. When she was out, he placed her in his car and drove to the woods. I met him here, he loaded her into my wagon after I placed a collar around her neck, and we brought her back here. I knew witches had magical properties so to be on the safe side, I drew the symbols you see there on the floor to effectively block her magic."

"I began giving her transfusions of my blood. It had no ill effects on Johann, so I wanted to see what it would do to her."

"A few days later, he caught the leprechaun. It's my understanding he's allergic to gold and that just wouldn't do. I began him on blood transfusions as well, combining a tiny bit of my blood with the witch's blood. If I could cure him of his ailment as I'd done with Johann, I'd be a hero!"

"How can you be so cruel? How can you call yourself a doctor? Doctors don't abuse and experiment on living beings. They help them. You're the monster here, not them," I ground out while pointing around the room.

"Ms. Woodson, experimentation is the way we learn so that we *can* help others. Doctors have been doing that very thing for centuries and look at all the progress we've made, the diseases we've cured! All the modern miracles brought about by experimenting. Sometimes we're successful, sometimes there are, unfortunately, casualties. But it's all in the name of science! And I am trying to help these wayward creatures. Didn't you hear a word I've said?"

"But you're forcing people to become lab experiments. They aren't here of their own free will, otherwise you wouldn't have to keep them locked in cages. Don't you have any empathy for what you're putting them through?"

"Ms. Woodson, have you ever been inside a medical laboratory? They have mice, rats, dogs, rabbits, monkeys. Do you honestly think any of them just walked in off the street one day and decided to sign up to be studied? And do you think those subjects roam freely about the labs? And, as any scientist will tell you, you can't allow your emotions to get in the way. You absolutely cannot become emotionally attached to your subjects. Emotions and science are not compatible. That was a huge mistake on my part with Frank and Elsa and look how that turned out."

"You should consider joining me in my cause. We'd gain fame and notoriety among science scholars. We'd be pioneers in a field never before heard of. Of course, my name would be the one on every scientist's lips. You, of course, would receive honorable mention."

"Have you thoroughly thought about this? Do you realize what trouble you would bring to these people's doorsteps? The danger you could create for their families by disclosing their true nature? What happens when someone decides they're something to fear? What happens when normals start hunting them? Are you really going to sacrifice these people for your own fame?"

"Ahh, Ms. Woodson! Greatness does not come without a few sacrifices. It's just the price one must pay to achieve overall success."

"Why were you following Gracie and me? Everywhere we went, you showed up?"

"I was curious as to what you were, especially when you took up with the other monsters quite quickly. When Johann called me and told me a girl and her talking dog were moving into town, it was exciting! We weren't sure what type of being you were, but the dog would be a fabulous subject to take on as a side project. Imagine if I could unlock the secret of talking animals! Hordes of pet owners would flock to me for treatment to allow their pets to speak to them! Sadly, as it turns out, you're just a mere human. If you don't join forces with me, I really have no use for you."

"You're despicable, Mr. Frankenstein."

"*Doctor* Frankenstein," he corrected me.

"You don't deserve that honor or that title. You're crazy."

"I see, Ms. Woodson, that you don't understand what I'm doing here, what great things I'm attempting to accomplish. Very well, then. You can join your friends. Now that I know where they are, I plan to get Elsa and Frank back. I will take Elsa next. Then it will be just a matter of time before Frank comes looking for her. When he does, I will be ready. I will take him and when the time is right, he, Elsa, and I will leave you to this town and its monsters."

"Of course, they will need to be contained once again until I'm sure I can trust them not to run away. Who knows? Maybe I'll just destroy Frank and keep Elsa. Frank is a flawed creation anyway. Elsa, though. Elsa is perfect! She will come to realize in time that she is better than Frank. She will then see she doesn't need him. I can create more like her, now that I've perfected the process. Just imagine it, if you will! An entire world filled with perfect specimens of the human race. And it will be all thanks to me! I'll go down in history as the one who did this. The father of the perfect human!"

"Meanwhile, you and your friends will be trapped here since no one knows this place exists and I will be long gone. It may take years before this place is discovered. By then, most, if not all of you will be nothing more than piles of bones."

The doctor rose, laughing maniacally.

"It's been a pleasure, Ms. Woodson. Too bad you wouldn't assist me in my journey of discovery."

"Beth! Run!" howled Gracie.

Chapter Nineteen

I jumped up from my chair as Walter stood and approached me. I saw he had pulled a filled hypodermic needle from his pocket.

"Be still, my dear. This won't hurt, just a little prick. Then you can take a nice nap."

I picked up my chair and heaved it over my shoulder as I started backing away.

"Don't you come near me with that," I yelled.

"Come on Ms. Woodson. It wouldn't be in your best interest to anger me."

He put the needle back in his lab coat pocket and picked up the shock collar remote from his desk.

"Hmmmm....eeny, meeny, miney, moe. Who will be the first to go? Or should I just hit the master switch and fry them all? If I do, that will end the suffering you seem to be convinced they are enduring and prevent them from dying of starvation after I leave. See, Ms. Woodson? I do have a heart." Again with the maniacal laughter.

I threw the chair at Walter. It caused him to lose his grip on the remote and it fell to the top of the desk. I had created enough of a distraction to buy me what I'd hoped was enough time to make a run for the trap door. Everyone was yelling and screaming as I raced toward the steps and scrambled up. Walter had paused to put the remote in the pocket opposite the pocket the needle was in. I was almost at the top of the stairs when Walter grabbed my ankle and started dragging me back down to the floor. The rough concrete scraped my stomach. My chin hit a couple of steps which caused me to bite my tongue. I bounced off every step on the way down to the floor.

I started screaming, Gracie was barking, Derek and the others being held captive were all yelling, except Johann who was laughing hysterically.

Walter managed to wrestle me to the floor, flipping me over onto my back and sat on top of me, pinning my legs. Between the wild sleigh ride down the steps on my stomach and him sitting on me, it was hard to breathe. I could taste the blood in my mouth from where I bit my tongue, almost gagging. He pulled the needle out again and I struggled against him, doing everything I could to keep him from sticking me with that needle. With me struggling against him, he wasn't able to hold onto both of my arms with one hand, keeping his other hand free to stick me, so I used that to my advantage.

He succeeded in securing one of my arms, but I struck out with the other. I managed to knock the needle from his hand and when he bent to the side to pick it up, I grabbed the key ring hanging on his belt as I bucked him off of me. He landed on his side next to me, but that little acrobatic stunt caused a sharp pain to shoot through my ribs. I'd managed to pull the keys loose and threw them in the vicinity of Derek's cage as hard as I could. Without Walter sitting on my abdomen, it wasn't hard to breathe. Now it just *hurt* to breathe.

"Now I'm angry, Ms. Woodson. You will pay for that little outburst."

He rolled off of his side, rose to his knees, then reached over to retrieve the needle. Of course it didn't shatter when it hit the floor. He started to pull the shock collar remote from his pocket, but I managed to kick it out of his hand. When it hit the floor, it broke into several pieces, rendering it useless. Sure! Couldn't have been two for two! Now he was so mad, his face seemed to be turning purple and a large vein popped out on his forehead.

As I was trying to get up on my feet, Walter pounced on top of me again, causing me to fall back down. Sitting astride me, Walter slapped me hard enough to cause my head to jerk to the side, dazing me. As I was trying to unscramble my brain from the force of his blow, he decided to jab the needle into my leg. As the needle made contact with my skin, there was a loud crash from upstairs. Footsteps started thundering across the floor. With the last bit of my strength, I let out a scream that would have made me famous in a Hollywood horror movie. Then everything went black.

Chapter Twenty

I awoke to a cool compress on my forehead and felt someone holding my hand. Next, I felt a rough tongue licking my face. I cracked an eye open to see I was in a hospital room and surrounded by a lot of people wearing anxious, but expectant looks on their faces. I'm amazed the doctors allowed this many people in someone's room. Gracie, seeing I was awake, started kissing my face in earnest. I laughed and moved my head to the side.

"Ow! That hurts! Everything hurts. Gracie, honey! Please stop!" I giggled and winced from the pain.

My voice was scratchy, and my throat felt like I'd swallowed a bowl of sand. Elsa poured some water into a glass from the pitcher next to my bed, placed a straw in it and handed it to Anna. She held the straw to my mouth so I could get a much-needed drink.

"Easy does it, sweetie. Just take a few small sips. "

"I'm so glad to see you! You saved us. Oh, how I've missed you!" Gracie said.

She started licking my face again and wiggled her whole body so much it felt like there was an earthquake happening on the bed. Every jolt sent a shockwave of pain through my ribs and my head.

"Gracie, please! Settle down," I said to her. "I'm fine."

I looked around the room to see Bart and Loralee, Francesca, Elsa, Frank, Jerry, and Guiseppe all looking at me smiling. Anna was sitting next to my bed, holding my hand. Once my eyes opened, she immediately sent a text to someone then jumped up to go get the doctor to inform him I was awake. She, Elsa, and Francesca had tears streaming down their faces. Everyone started talking at once.

I laughed and slowly sat up in bed, wincing with every movement, as I said, "Okay, everyone. One at a time."

Everyone took turns hugging me and telling me how glad they were I was okay. Once Anna came back in, she immediately went back to her bedside chair, took my hand once more, refusing to let go. At least Gracie had finally settled down next to me and stopped bouncing around. The jackhammer in my head was thankfully easing up as well.

Bart began, "Ms. Beth, I am mighty pleased to see you. I was sorely afraid you were running off and going to get yourself kilt. We found out why I couldn't enter the cabin. The doctor had poured Dead Sea salt all around the house, in the windowsills, and over the door. That's a sure way to keep ghosts from coming in or getting out in Loralee's case. Guess those two planned ahead for everything. All this time, that crazy doctor has been holding my beautiful Loralee against her will. Just burns me up inside. I wish I would have gone looking for Loralee a heck of a lot sooner. We mighta found each other before that madman took her."

Bart had certainly blossomed since our first meeting. He seemed to possess so much more confidence than he did when I first met him. I hadn't noticed any M&M piles lately.

Francesca spoke up and started telling me what had happened after I was stuck with Walter's needle.

"When you snagged the keys from Walter and threw them, they landed right by Derek's cage. While you wrestled with Walter, he was distracted long enough for Derek to take off his belt, throw one end through the bars and get the keys. He didn't want to risk Walter shocking him again, not knowing the remote had gotten broken in the fight. He managed to hook the keys with his belt buckle, slide them over and unlock his cage."

"As Walter started to jab the needle into your leg, Derek ran toward Walter and tackled him, knocking him off of you, unfortunately not before Walter stuck you and the drug took effect. Walter didn't have any more needles on him, and he wasn't much of a match for Derek, especially without the remote. It took every ounce of willpower Derek possessed to stop from killing Walter."

"Meanwhile, Jerry, Frank and Guiseppe had arrived at the cabin with Bart leading the way. They kicked in the front door, then heard all the noise coming from below. They found the way in, thanks to your scream, and saw Derek fighting with Walter. Giuseppe tended to you, Jerry joined in to help Derek, as Frank searched for something to tie Walter up with. He found some zip ties and, once Derek had Walter under control, Derek hog-tied the doctor to subdue him until back up arrived."

Giuseppe continued the story. "After Walter was secured, Derek started opening all the cages of the people Walter had captured, except Johann. He removed the collars everyone was wearing, except for the mayor. Seems he was in cahoots with Walter, helping him lure unsuspecting people in for Walter's experiments. Derek put Walter in a cage for added security."

"Loralee was understandably frightened and wouldn't leave her cage. It took an entire bucket of holy water to remove the Dead Sea salt from on and around her cage so that she could be freed. We managed to clear enough salt from around the cabin door to let Bart enter. When she saw Bart, that's all it took to convince her she was safe."

"Frank went outside to call the council and an ambulance. The council showed up and took Walter and Johann away. Once the paramedics checked the others over, we took Seamus, Francesca, and Mrs. Goody home."

"Fortunately," Jerry added, "the symbols trapping Mrs.

Goody were written in chalk so they were easily removed."

"Where is Derek now?" I asked.

"He had to go with the council to give a statement," Anna answered. "He saw what that madman did to you, Beth. It enraged him so much to see Walter hurting you that I think had Jerry, Giuseppe, and Frank not been there, Derek probably would have killed him."

"When he saw you were being loaded into the ambulance and taken in for observation, he followed the ambulance all the way to the hospital and stayed there until he was 100% sure you were okay. It was only after hearing you were banged up, but okay, that he left, albeit begrudgingly, to give his statement to the council."

"What he did, not immediately reporting to the council, instead choosing to go with you to the hospital is against council protocol so he might have to face repercussions from them for his actions."

"I don't want him to get in trouble because of me, Anna. Do you think they'll let me speak with them?"

"It will be okay, Beth. Derek has an exemplary record and I'm sure the council will just give him a reminder. If he does get some sort of discipline out of this, I'll call my mother and they can deal with her!" Anna smiled. "Even the council doesn't want to go up against my mother when she feels her baby boy is being wronged!"

The thought of a bunch of stuffy councilmen going up against Mrs. Capaldi made me chuckle, which hurt tremendously.

"Was I hit by a semi or something? I hurt everywhere."

"You have two cracked ribs, a fractured wrist, lots of scrapes and bruises. They thought you might have a concussion, but thankfully you did not. You also have a black eye and a lot of facial swelling. I thought I'd tell you that before you see a mirror. You are so lucky this is all you have. From what I've heard that fight was brutal. You held your own though." Elsa leaned over and kissed my cheek. "We are all so glad you're here, Beth!"

"We don't know how to thank you, Beth," Frank said. "You found all of our missing people and helped stop my creator, I'm ashamed to say, from doing further harm to us."

"I feel it's my fault Walter was here. Elsa and I noticed he seemed to be slipping further and further into madness. We weren't sure what his plans for us were, but we were getting worried. We spoke about things at night after Walter had gone to bed. We made plans and decided at the first opportunity, we would escape. That day he left us alone, we knew opportunity was upon us and we left."

"We bounced around from town to town for many years, trying to stay hidden from Walter by blending into the community we were in at the time. Trying hard to not bring attention to ourselves and never staying too long in one place. One day we stumbled onto this town. We both felt like we were finally home. We felt safe here. We'd hoped after all the years that had passed, Walter had given up searching for us, so we settled here and built our life together."

"Again, thank you, Beth. Elsa and I will never be able to repay you for all you've done. Almost sacrificing yourself in the process. Had something happened to you at the hands of that madman, I could have never forgiven myself."

Giuseppe spoke up, "And thank you for saving my beautiful Francesca. I don't know what I would have done if I'd lost her."

"Frank, Guiseppe, you don't have to thank me. I know I've only been here a short while, but I care about you." I looked around the room. "All of you! And it's not your fault. Walter was crazy. You and Elsa had nothing to do with that. You couldn't have predicted what he was going to do. That he would come here looking for you but decide instead to start experimenting on others."

"Thank you, Beth. Just know you have my sincerest gratitude. All of us thank you!"

"So, what will happen to Walter and Johann now?" I asked.

"The council doesn't condone behavior such as theirs. They will be dealt with swiftly and justly. We won't have to worry about them ever coming around here again," Francesca answered.

We started talking about things until Elsa finally said, "I think we all need to go and let Beth get some rest. She's had a hard day."

Everyone agreed and came over to me one by one to carefully hug me, being mindful of my injuries, and thank me for all I'd done. Anna was going to stick around to see what the doctor had to say after he examined me. I was hoping to just go home where I'd be more comfortable.

Bart and Loralee hung back after everyone else left and Anna had gone out to see what was taking the doctor so long.

Bart was now surrounded by a pink glow, which intertwined with Loralee's matching pink glow.

"Miss Beth, I would like to formally introduce you to the love of my life, my Loralee. Loralee, this is my friend, Miss Beth."

"It's a pleasure to meet you, Miss Beth. Thank you so much for saving me from that horrible brute and reuniting me with my beloved Bart. I have missed him so over these years."

"I figured you'd gone on without me, but Miss Beth wouldn't let me give up." He placed a small kiss on Loralee's cheek.

"Bart, I would never have left without you. You are my love."

Bart smiled. "And you are mine. Again, thank you, Miss Beth."

"I'm so glad you two are reunited. But you are the real hero of the story, Bart! He was so brave, Loralee! Without his help, none of us would be here right now."

Bart's glow changed to a deep crimson color.

"Miss Beth..." he began.

"Seriously Bart. You were the one to get help and lead them to where we were. Please allow ME to thank YOU!"

Bart hung his head bashfully as Loralee placed a kiss on his cheek.

"My brave and wonderful love," she said.

"Miss Beth, I do have one small favor to ask?"

"Sure, Bart, anything."

"Well, Loralee and I have talked it over and would like to ask, if it's not too much trouble, if we can stay at the house. You and Gracie are so great to be around, and we'd love to stay if you'll have us. We won't be any trouble."

"Of course, Bart, Loralee! Gracie and I would be honored to share our home with you, right Gracie?"

"You bet, Bart. Without you, the house wouldn't be here. It will be your home for as long as you both would like to stay."

"Much obliged, ma'am, Gracie."

"Thank you ever so kindly!"

"Okay, Loralee, let's go and let Miss Beth get some rest. If you need us for anything once you get home, you just give us a holler," and, with that, Bart and Loralee popped out.

Anna found the doctor. He checked me over one final time, then begrudgingly signed off on the release papers after giving me a prescription for mild painkillers as well as home care instructions. They wheeled me down to the exit where Anna was waiting to take me home. Getting up in her SUV was a bit difficult, but I finally managed with help from Anna and the nurse who wheeled me down. I was securely belted in and more than ready to go home!

Chapter Twenty-One

An hour or so later, Gracie and I were relaxing on the couch watching television when there was a knock on the door. I got up and slowly hobbled to the door to see who was there. I looked through the peephole and saw Derek standing on my porch. I opened the door and invited him in. He was still in his uniform and looked pretty tired.

"Good evening, Ms. Woodson," he began.

"Beth, please, Derek. After all that's happened, there's really no need for formality."

"Okay, Beth. I just wanted to stop by on my way home and see how you are and to offer my sincerest thanks for your help solving this case."

"I'm fine, Derek. A little sore, banged up, and tired, but I'm glad to be home and really glad Gracie is back."

"I'm glad to be back, Beth," Gracie agreed.

"I'm glad to hear it. But do you realize how much danger you put yourself in today? You're lucky to be alive."

"I do, *Deputy Capaldi*, but I helped save your butt, didn't I?" I shot back.

"I didn't come here to fight, Beth. I was worried about you. Seeing you fighting with that madman and being helpless to do anything…. it's something I never want to experience again."

"Did you ever find out how Walter was able to evade you when you were tracking him?"

"Yes, I did. That was one of the things that frustrated me. I'd get the scent then, bam, it's gone. Walter was, above all else, an inventor. He's the one who created those shock collars and the remote that operated individual collars or a group. It just depended on what button he pushed. Somehow, he was able to create a masking spray. Once he sprayed it on whatever he was trying to hide, the scent trail disappeared. It's too bad he's one of the bad guys. He has brains and can create some very interesting gadgets."

"And that empty canister you found? Turns out it was a Dead Sea salt bomb. That's why Bart froze and couldn't follow Walter that day he took Gracie."

I softened. "It all worked out in the end. I'm a little worse for wear, but it's over now and I'll be back up on my feet in no time. So, tell me what happened with the council. Anna mentioned you'd broken protocol and it would be addressed by the council. You didn't get into any trouble over it, did you?"

"The council interviewed me after speaking with Walter and Johann. They discussed, voted, and agreed behind closed doors, the best punishment for those two would be to imprison them in the Nether for the rest of their lives. They'll never be a threat to us or anyone ever again. As for me, they merely gave me a warning. But they were all smiling when they did, so it's nothing. Nothing will go into my employee files about protocol, so it's all good."

"How did they get Walter and Johann to confess?"

"When you're in the presence of the council, you are unable to lie. If a question is directed toward you, you have to and will tell the truth. It's kind of a failsafe method to assist the council with determining the level of sentencing you receive for minor infractions or full out crimes. It also prevents the council from making bogus convictions or overly harsh sentences because, say, a witness lied. It doesn't matter which side of the law you're on either. You are compelled to be truthful. They both sang their hearts out when asked about their activities."

"That's a relief. What's the Nether? Sorry! I know I'm asking a lot of questions."

"No, it's fine. It's sort of the equivalent of purgatory for magical beings or some non-magicals who have grossly harmed magicals. Those sentenced there never get to move on to anything beyond it. It's a place completely devoid of everything. No color, music; no day or night. Nothing. Worst of all, magical beings are always sentenced to go there alone and stripped of any and all magic they possess. The Nether is the most extreme punishment the council can dole out. You have to be a true monster to receive sentencing like that. And it's a life-long sentence. Once the council sentences you there, you can never leave."

"That's good to hear, Derek."

"Johann was the one who left the note under your door. Oh, and one of the deputies pulled a car over tonight for speeding and driving recklessly. Seems it was your ex-husband and a female companion by the name of Paula Yates, aka Elizabeth Lynn Woodson. She was completely naked, and he was close to being the same. Both had been drinking at Seamus's Pot of Gold, the bar here in town. Seamus was one of Walter's captives. As soon as he was free, he headed straight to the bar to go back to work."

"Your ex-husband kept insisting he'd only had two beers and his friend had one margarita. The only problem is the alcohol is ten times stronger here than it is in outside communities to non-magicals. Two beers here is the equivalent of about two cases in 'normal', nonmagical bars. One margarita equals a full bottle of straight tequila. He and his companion, along with their dog, were taken to jail here in town. Your ex and his friend will be transferred to the county jail tomorrow morning. He confessed to trashing your car."

"The funny thing is, Paula was one of my closest friends. You're telling me neither she nor my ex-husband knew my real name?!? Amazing! And that poor dog! The sights it must have seen! But what will happen to it?"

"I think Anna and Jerry are taking the dog. Daisy has been wanting a dog forever. Daisy has even named the dog. Casey, she said, because it rhymed with Gracie and they're both Aussie mixes. You've made quite an impression on my niece. She acts like you hung the moon and she's more than willing to howl up at it. Sorry, a little were humor."

"Why, Officer Capaldi! I do believe you just made a punny," I chuckled.

"Stick around. There are plenty more lousy puns yet to come."

Derek smiled and I'd swear I heard a heavenly choir singing. Down girl!

"Also, I'm sorry I misjudged you, Beth. Anna informed me I'd, in her own words, 'completely, totally, and single-handedly ruined your birthday' and I had 'better come up with a plan to remedy that' or she was telling Mama! So, when you're feeling better, I plan to make things up to you."

He brought his hand up toward my face like he was going to touch my cheek, but then thought better of it and dropped his hand back to his side. Right now, the tenderness in his eyes alone was enough to make me melt into a puddle of goo. Had he touched me, I probably would have levitated.

"Anyway, take care. The town owes you. *I* owe you. If you ever need anything, you have my number."

"Thanks Derek. Drive safe. Goodnight."

I closed the door and looked at Gracie.

"Okay, girl, what do you say we head to bed?"

"Yes, and Beth? I love you."

"And I you, my Gracie girl."

Epilogue

A few weeks later, the town was gearing up for a celebration. Guiseppe and Francesca, along with Frank and Elsa, decided to throw a party in my honor at Seamus's Pot of Gold. I told them a party really wasn't necessary, but they'd insisted. All the town was coming tonight. My ribs were still bandaged, but most of the swelling had gone down and the bruises I had on my face and body were getting lighter. My car was still trashed, so Derek was coming to pick me up and escort me to tonight's festivities.

Seamus willingly held the party at his bar. He told me I could have free drinks for life, although knowing what I now knew about the alcohol here, I wasn't sure I'd be taking him up on his offer any time soon. He assured me he had normal beer and wine stashed in the back collecting dust. Apparently a little good came out of Walter's psychotic experiments. Seamus was no longer allergic to gold.

We were planning a summer wedding for Bart and Loralee. They asked if they could hold the ceremony at my house. I readily agreed. Loralee asked if I'd be her maid of honor. Gracie would serve as ring bearer.

Derek was offered the position of interim mayor by the council, but he respectfully turned them down. He told them he felt he was more useful keeping the streets of Raven's Glen safe than sitting behind a desk. They offered the position to the soon-to-be retiring sheriff, and he accepted, making sure the council knew he was only taking it on a temporary basis.

After much discussion, Frank decided to run for mayor once the council announced the election. I knew he'd be great in the position and really hoped he would win. Elsa wasn't sure what they would do with the market if he did win, but Frank assured her their current store manager would gladly step up and take on more responsibility for the day-to-day operation. I'm not sure he's fully convinced Elsa, but she seems to be coming around.

It turns out the other missing being held in Walter's lab, Mrs. Goody, was the witch I'd gotten Gracie from. The strange symbols in front of her cage were sigils—some sort of ancient symbols that rendered her witchcraft useless.

Derek had arrived to pick me up and I was just getting ready to walk out the door with him, when my phone rang. I looked at the display and saw *'Grandma'*.

"Oh, lord, what's she getting up to now?" I asked as I pushed the button to answer.

"Bethie Lynn, it's Grandma. Hey, listen, I think I'm going to take you up on that offer to come visit."

"Great, Grams! When do you want to come?"

"In about two hours. I'm at the airport now. The fuzz is breathing down my neck and I need to leave town, let the heat die down a little."

"What?!? Grams, what did you do?"

"I'll see you soon, sweetie. Bye." <click>

The end....or is it?

About The Author

Wendy Dunkin

Hi all! This book was a labor of love. Or insanity. Not sure which. This is my first try at writing and I thoroughly understand when my author friends say these characters get in your head and won't shut up! (Yeah, that's the story we'll stick with for the voices in our heads!)

I've read books for as far back as I can remember and one of my mom's favorite stories about me was when I was three and sat my beloved grandmother down so I could read to her. I read her the book cover to cover. My grandmother, thinking I'm a super intelligent child prodigy, exclaimed to my mom, "She can read!" My mom, always willing to out me told her, "She can read because she's heard the book so many times, she's memorized it."

Thanks mom!

I'm a postal worker by trade; a poet at heart. I love to travel, rehab old houses, sing karaoke, and hang out with my animals, kids, their spouses and my adorabaly spoiled (by me!) grandson.

I live in the midwest with my own non-speaking Aussie mix and three cats, one of whom my dog adopted. Never a dull moment in my house.

Thanks for reading.

Made in the USA
Monee, IL
04 September 2023